It was time to pay the piper

Mack Bolan did as he was told. It was suicide to do otherwise. He knew that Dandridge wouldn't kill him immediately. Guys like him liked to gloat first. There was a ritual that had to be observed. There'd be questions and torture.

The Executioner had to figure he'd worked up quite a tab over the years interfering with and actively opposing Company operations around the world. He had gone up against more than his fair share of CIA agents, as well. The fact that those agents were a disgrace to the country they'd theoretically been serving was no consolation.

To Dandridge's way of thinking, the tab was long overdue....

MACK BOLAN ®
The Executioner

DON PENDLETON'S
THE EXECUTIONER®
LEVIATHAN

A GOLD EAGLE BOOK FROM
WORLDWIDE®

TORONTO • NEW YORK • LONDON
AMSTERDAM • PARIS • SYDNEY • HAMBURG
STOCKHOLM • ATHENS • TOKYO • MILAN
MADRID • WARSAW • BUDAPEST • AUCKLAND

First edition November 2001
ISBN 0-373-64276-8

Special thanks and acknowledgment to
Gerald Montgomery for his contribution to this work.

LEVIATHAN

By Names and Images are all powers awakened and reawakened.

> —From the Neophyte Initiation Ritual,
> *The Order of Stella Matutina*

There is no autonomy in wielding absolute power among men. Even the men who consider themselves untouchable serve some kind of master. Everyone is accountable.

> —Mack Bolan

For those who dare.
We salute you.

Prologue

King Edward VII
Memorial Hospital, Bermuda

Linda Larson had been a nurse for thirteen years and a member of the cult since conception. Nobody in proper society would have suspected her dark faith, and there were a few of that lot as well who were members of the old religion and had been as far back as family genealogies could be traced. Her attendance at the Anglican cathedral in Hamilton was a perfect record. No Bermudan who attended Mass there could ever recall not seeing her in the same pew on any given Sunday. Always wearing something bright and breezy with a subtle undercurrent of deliberate Eros. It was a detail about her that didn't escape the notice of every male parishioner with a pulse.

For a thirty-nine-year-old woman, she still had more sizzle and juice than women half her age. Yet she seldom seemed to be in the company of a man. When she was, that man was always Wesson Fairchild, chairman of the Bermuda Conservatory. Fairchild was a weathered flagship of a man. Dark eyes and raven hair with silver streaks through the temples. Deep lines etched his forehead and cheeks, like precise knife cuts.

To Larson, Wesson Fairchild was much more than a

lover or a surrogate father figure. To her, Fairchild was a god. His every word and command was a direct utterance from something that didn't know death and had been around since before the universe even existed.

Fairchild was the all-father to the cult. The one duty every cultist shared, despite rank or standing, was that of vigilance. Watch for the clues. Watch for the signs. For the time was near. Soon the veil between the realities would be astrologically weakest and then the gateway would open to let *it* back into this world. Or so the cult was indoctrinated to believe.

What Larson was seeing now was like ambrosial delight. The blood, the screaming, the confusion, the chaos. It was like a banquet to her. The first sortie of helicopters had flown in from the north over the dark Atlantic, and began landing in the parking lots and lawns that surrounded the only large hospital in Bermuda.

Larson was outside the emergency-room entrance, leaning against the wall and smoking a menthol light cigarette when the airspace above the hospital campus thundered with the wash and wind of ten helicopters landing in a big horseshoe perimeter from north to south around the emergency wing.

The helicopters were immaculately restored UH-1 Hueys bought surplus from the U.S. government at pennies on the dollar. The workhorse birds were painted midnight blue and white—the "national" colors of the legally recognized city-state at sea whose name and symbol was the constellation of Cassiopeia. The pilots stayed on the ground long enough for all personnel to disembark before jerking the helicopters straight back up into the night and out to sea again, heading due north for another load of human cargo.

There were only five casualties with this lift, and the

chopper had landed right on the ramp outside the emergency-room entrance. A second bird landed to the rear of the first, and ten more Cassiopeia medical people joined the five pulling off litters as the door gunner unsnapped the quick-release buckles on the straps that secured the litters to the deck during the flight.

There would be three more sorties before the job could be called done and the mission tempo relaxed at all.

Larson ran into the hospital at first sight of the casualties.

"Prepare for triage!" she yelled toward the nursing station. "Five, maybe more casualties!"

Things were hopping to life back there, but she didn't have time to supervise that. She was outside again and almost collided with the first litter in the race to get the casualties into the hospital and receiving treatment. The look on the two medics' faces told Larson that every second counted.

She sidestepped out of the way and took the IV bag from the guy pulling up the rear.

"Boating accident?" she asked.

The two medics trotted through the double automatic glass doors and into the waiting room.

"To your left!" she directed.

The rear guy laughed harshly. "No propeller does that to a man."

The medic's accent was American, eastern seaboard. Probably New York.

She was removing blankets and blood-soaked bandages to get a better visual assessment of the man's wounds. The burning, super-mentholated stench of ammonia assaulted her nostrils. It was an odor intimately familiar to the one-half of the population who scrubbed the floors for the other half. It was a stench that Larson knew from another…more organic source. She knew what it meant to smell that rare stench, radiating off a barely living body flown in from out there on the open waters.

She had to get word to the others.

She handed the IV bag to a young intern she thought was good enough to eat, but he wasn't one of the Chosen, and smiled at him.

"We'll need a lot more blood. I'll be off to stores!"

She backed off as hospital emergency staff wheeling a gurney intercepted the litter. The Cassiopeia medics placed the litter on the gurney, and the mauled victim was rolled under a hanging examination light. The young intern passed the IV responsibility to the first nurse to join his side of the gurney. A seasoned doctor took over the triage.

Larson stood back and couldn't budge until she saw the condition of the first body. It would confirm or deny everything.

The blankets and swaddling were removed. What was left of the human being underneath by all counts should have been dead already. From blood loss and shock alone. The guy was young, probably in his midtwenties.

The nurse holding the IV bag was having a hard time with the smell. She coughed and tried to keep her composure in the face of the emergency.

"What's that smell? It's horrible!"

The victim's physical condition was even more of a challenge to cool-headed professionalism. Whatever order of life the attacker belonged to, its methods weren't clean and surgical like a shark's. Whatever this nightmare was, it was designed to grind flesh and bone into pulp. The man's right leg had been seized, then spun counterclockwise until muscle, bone and flesh tore apart and separated. The ragged stump at the hip flexor had been savagely constricted with a makeshift tourniquet to keep the femoral artery from letting what little was left of his liquid life from spraying away. The man's left arm was gone, as was most of the shoulder into the collarbone. The arm had been bitten off by something roughly V-shaped, with serrated edges, like teeth on a steak knife. The bite radius was an easy eight inches across. The wound had been cauterized sloppily but with something very hot. Probably a blow torch.

The man's bloodied torso was covered in ugly, discolored purple-bluish bruises in the shape of rings. Each ring was about the size of a teacup saucer. The flesh was broken in places around the edge of the rings suggesting again, serrated edges. In the center of some of the rings were deep puncture wounds, as if some kind of bony hook had lodged into the flesh, to irrevocably hold its prey in that deadly embrace until consumed.

Larson had seen enough. She was light-headed with excitement. The others had to be told. The senior physician looked up briefly and saw her standing there with a glazed look on her face.

"Nurse! Weren't you going to go get blood from stores?"

She nodded quickly and spun away from the bedlam of the emergency room. She ran past the public elevators. A lone janitor was polishing the floor with an electric buffer. She went to the bank of public phones and plucked the handset off the cradle. She had chosen the privacy partitioned pay phone in the middle of the line. She deposited her coins and dialed.

The line rang once.

The other end was picked up immediately, and a man's resonant voice answered.

"Yes?"

"The stars are right," Larson announced.

Then she hung up the phone and went to look for some blood.

1

Georgetown, Maryland

Leo Turrin was well aware that he was being shadowed. He hadn't spotted any foot pursuit, but the car was always there behind him, staying a half block back, pulling to the curb when Turrin stopped moving to let his salt-and-pepper schnauzer investigate an odor in a bush or do his business on a conveniently located tree.

The car was a big black late model Cadillac. The paint job seemed to glow in the dying sunlight of the early evening. Turrin had a good idea who the occupants were in that car. He just couldn't understand why they would be following him.

Turrin had "retired" from Family life a long time ago, back when the Stony Man program was just being born. He'd been an underboss of western Massachusetts back in the day and an undercover operative for the Justice Department. It was a heady and dangerous act to try to balance. He'd almost lost the juggle on one occasion and would have had it not been for one hellfire guy named Mack Bolan.

Turrin missed those cowboy days sometimes. This day wasn't one of them. He spent his days now riding a desk in the Justice Department doing administrative stuff and keeping his fingers in the organized crime pie only enough to keep the lines of information flowing for intelligence purposes. It was a more relaxed existence now, a safer one to be sure. But an old dog like Turrin hadn't survived undercover as long as he had by forgetting certain simple truths.

Never let your guard down.

He wondered what the stalking black Caddy might be the harbinger of. The guys in that car had to know that he'd made them. If it was a hit, they would have moved on him right from the start. No dicking around playing tag. Which meant that these boys had some other reason to be following a retired Mob chieftain walking his dog in a quiet neighborhood of brownstones and walk-ups in well-to-do Georgetown on a spring evening.

Turrin was armed. He was packing his pistol inside the waistband of his Chino slacks, underneath the light windbreaker he wore over his golf shirt. It was a Smith & Wesson Chiefs .38 Special snub-nosed revolver with a 5-round cylinder. The weapon was loaded with Glaser safety slugs, which were absolutely horrific in terms of stopping power. But the rounds were practically useless against an assailant wearing a vest. If it came to a shootout with these guys, they were probably wearing vests. He'd have to concentrate on neck shots or limb shots.

But the little Fed's guts were telling him it wouldn't come to that. Not this night.

The game of tag had to have been losing its appeal. The occupants of the Caddy were taking a more proactive posture now. The big car powered away from the curb and cruised past Turrin to the end of the block, where the car signaled right and turned, immediately sliding in next to the curb. The unseen wheelman put the transmission into park and left the engine running.

Now the ball was in Turrin's court. He could turn tail and walk the other way, or he could keep going down the block. Even in retirement, the little Fed couldn't display cowardice. That's not the way the game was played. He had a reputation still among the very few left alive in the Families that had survived the Bolan wars. He couldn't let word get around that his old nickname was really his true stripe: *Pussy.* Turrin came up in the ranks running girls. Black book. High-class call girls to entrap the rich and the influential.

If he was wrong about this, if it really was a clever hit, he had no choice now but to walk right into it.

"Let's go, Simba. Come on, boy. Let's hear what the nasty men have to say."

Turrin put on his best poker face and walked the rest of the way down the block in no particular hurry. He decided to turn right at the corner rather than drag this out by crossing the street and forcing the car to make a second try at intercepting him. Turrin watched the car out of the corner of his eye, acting as if its presence were of no concern to him. As he came abreast of the big Caddy, the rear curbside window powered down and an immaculately dressed man leaned out.

"Mr. Turrin, sir. May I have a moment of your time?"

The guy had headcock written all over him. He nudged somebody sitting in the passenger seat up front but invisible behind tinted glass.

"Sal! Get out of the car and take Mr. Turrin's dog for him. So he can join me and we can talk like men."

The door on the shotgun side opened and a big Mob

soldier in an Armani suit exited the car. He adjusted his tie and looked both ways out of habit. He closed his door and stepped up next to Turrin, towering over him.

"Mr. Turrin, it would be my great honor to walk your dog for you, sir. While you talk to my boss about business."

Turrin looked from Sal to the headcock framed in the rear window.

"Maybe I can save you gentlemen some time," Turrin said. "I'm not in the Outfit full-time anymore, see?"

"Mr. Turrin, please, let Sal take your dog and just hear what I have to say. That's all I'm asking."

Turrin looked up at the giant standing next to him, shrugged and handed him the leash. Sal and Simba strolled off together.

The door opened and the man inside moved to the opposite side of the bench seat to make room for his guest. When Turrin got into the car and closed the door, the mobster rolled up the window so their private talk could remain that way.

"I'm listening," Turrin said.

"Hey, Vincent," the headcock said to the driver. "Put the car in motion. Go around the block a few times or something."

Vincent nodded, shifted and pulled the luxury automobile away from the curb.

"Mr. Turrin, my name is Tony Pensi. I represent an offshore interest with a very delicate problem."

"What kind of problem?"

"Very unusual, sir. It's not like the kind of problem you can just solve the way we did back in the day, if you know what I mean?"

"You need some finesse, is what you're sayin'."

"Uh-huh. And when I was asked to assist in finding

the solution to this problem, everybody told me the same thing—find Leo. Leo Turrin is the man you need."

"I'm honored, really. But I'm not as well connected as I used to be."

"Sir, you're being modest."

"No, Mr. Pensi. I'm being honest."

"Everyone said you'd be straight up with me. That's why I want to deal with you on this."

Turrin felt that trying to be modest and underrate his reputation wasn't going to get him anywhere with this guy. His interest, however, was piqued.

"Okay, what's the problem? What do you need? And please call me Leo."

"As you well know, Leo, the organization has taken some setbacks in the last twenty years. We've had challengers, and we've had the Feds getting much better about building cases that shut down whole Families in one blow. We've had to diversify, go legit. Put our fingers into other pies—more ambiguous pies shall we say? We've had to forge new alliances while leaving other enterprises by the side for the spics and the spades to take over from us.

"We've been looking for new opportunities, new ways of doing what we've always been best at. Supplying man's craving for those things that society puts out of reach.

"Leo, I'm here today as an emissary, so to speak. The man I'm representing is not one of us. He isn't made. But he's got connections, got his feet into two different worlds, and he's brought the two together to give us something we never had before. Our own country."

Turrin wasn't sure he'd heard the man correctly. The little Fed wasn't at all in the loop on this one. Something like this was big. People talked about these things. He hadn't heard a peep through the grapevine.

"Repeat that last part, Tony. I'm not sure I understood you."

"We got a piece of our own country, Leo. It's a partnership in nation building. A truly glorious moment for us. The United Nations General Assembly has officially recognized this country of ours."

"I must have missed that news broadcast."

"Our partners don't like exposure. They would rather not have the world know of their sponsorship of this experiment. It represents a whole new frontier for us and our traditional money pots."

"What is this partnership you keep mentioning?"

"We've had a relationship with these people since the Bay of Pigs, Leo. The Company has its own share of problems these days, as we do. Congress holds their purse strings, and they don't like that. Making the world safe for American interests takes money and balls. Congress hasn't got the balls to do the job like it needs to be done. This has necessitated the Company moving into areas that have traditionally been our turf. Narcotics for example. The world's hunger for illegal drugs is never going to dry up. No matter how much the world's governments might try to legislate this hunger away. It only makes sense that our two organizations should come together like this for our mutual benefit. The Company benefits by receiving the monies they need to do their work around the globe, money that Congress has no control over. We benefit by operating manufacturing and sales in a place where the legal climate is entirely favorable to our enterprise. We make the laws there as all sovereign nations have the right to do within the boundaries of their national territory. That makes our operation untouchable. It's a legal tangle that completely hamstrings our enemies in Washington. We can't be raided out there, and we can't be invaded."

The undercover Fed in Leo Turrin was listening to all this with a growing sense of dread. It was the ultimate bad news: a rogue CIA getting in bed with La Cosa Nostra to found a nation where drug manufacturing and export were legally protected enterprises. Turrin knew of a certain someone who was going to want to know about this development immediately.

This guy didn't recognize national boundaries or sovereign claims to immunity.

"Where exactly is this new country located?"

"Thirty-one miles north of Bermuda in the Atlantic. Our new nation isn't a real piece of land in the traditional sense. We've acquired an offshore oil platform that was never completely constructed. The Jefferson Manhattan Oil Company for mysterious reasons abandoned it some years ago. It was taken off their books recently, and our partnership was formed by the man I am here representing today."

"And he is?"

"His name is Damien Cassandra. He's a lawyer by trade. Specializes in international law. The task of tackling the legalities of this experiment was his cup of tea from the very start."

"So what's the problem? Sounds to me like you've got a dream setup."

"Our problem is much more bizarre than hassles from the world community. We have a marine biology problem, Leo."

"Say again?"

"Mother Nature, that unpredictable bitch, has thrown us a curve ball no one could have anticipated. I believe I have an idea now why that platform was never completed. It seems to be the hunting grounds of something very dangerous, something very horrific. We're not quite sure exactly what it is, if it is one creature or several. But nothing can get in or out of Cassiopeia by water anymore. These things won't let that happen. You can see our lifeblood is access to our product. That access has to be by water. We're in the middle of the goddamn ocean. Most helicopters don't have the range without refueling. We need shipping traffic, or this great thing of ours is dead in the water. Pardon the pun."

Turrin laughed.

"So let me get this straight. You've got a sea monster and not the Colombians or Jamaicans muscling you on your own turf. Well, I don't know who told you I've got a degree in monster hunting, but I'm afraid I wouldn't know where to begin."

"What we really need, Leo, is discretion and quiet. We want experts to handle this neatly without a lot of attention. We don't want people being scared off by the deep-sea equivalent of the bogeyman. There's too much money at stake for that."

"What exactly do you think you need?"

"People who have no fear. Who will take big risks for big payoffs. We've lost most of our full-timers out there. They won't come back after the killing frenzy that went on last night. And we'll need experts in marine life to direct the fearless killers in how to best defeat our problem."

Turrin steepled his fingers and thought about it. He couldn't turn his back on this one. It was just too perfect an opportunity to disrupt something that needed disruption.

"How soon do you want to launch?"

"Within forty-eight hours. Time is money, *compadre*."

"What you offer here, Tony, is something I haven't had in a long time. A real challenge. I'll help you. When I have assembled the resources you need, how will I contact you?"

Pensi pulled a business card from inside his suit coat and handed it to Turrin. The undercover Fed studied it briefly, then pocketed the card.

He smiled broadly and said, "Take me back to my dog. I've got work to do."

AFTER TURRIN was dropped off, Pensi had his driver get on the freeway and head for Virginia. He made a call on his Company-issue cell phone equipped with scrambler and contacted his control.

"Yeah, it's me. It's a set. He took the bait. He had no idea that we weren't really wise guys."

"Excellent," the voice on the other end said. "When did he seem to think he would deliver the goods?"

"I gave him forty-eight hours."

"He'll be back to you in short order. His people will want to jump all over this."

"What do you want me to do in the meantime?"

"Baby-sit that phone. I want to know as soon as it's a go."

"You got it."

"Out here."

"Yeah, out."

Pensi killed the transmission and pocketed the spook gear.

"Hey, Vince," he said to the driver. "Let's find a seafood place and get a bite and a beer. I have a powerful hunger for red salmon right now."

Seafood, that was rich. Seafood was what a certain interfering bastard was going to end up becoming when the trap was sprung.

2

San Diego, California

The woman entered the office of John Gray Investigations like a whirlwind. Johnny Bolan Gray was working on the last mug of his third pot of java for the day when she burst through the front door. The office had no receptionist area, just an office, a desk and a back room that served as filing and storage. Johnny's office occupied one-half of what used to be a 7-11 store located in the rough side of town. A graveyard shift clerk had been robbed and murdered in the store, and 7-11 policy never allowed a store to reopen again if a clerk was killed during the commission of a violent crime. A "school" that trained the gullible for careers in pro wrestling rented the other half of the building.

The woman was young, eighteen to twenty-two years old, and moving with the motivation of the desperate. She was dressed in an emerald green gown that was slit up the side to her hip and white gloves that covered her arms up to the biceps. Her makeup and mascara were smeared from crying. Dirty blond hair was piled on top of her head in big curls and rings. A pearl choker encircled her neck. She was carrying her shoes, which looked

like a cross between black rubber high heels and a pair
of Doc Martens. She had on white hose with black
stripes, like the pattern convicts used to wear in old
movies.

The wild entrance caught Johnny by surprise. He
didn't say anything until she forced the glass door
closed and slid the dead bolt into place. He'd had the
floor-to-ceiling glass removed and real walls installed
in the front of the office. He didn't like all that glass.
Glass was easy to shoot through and even easier to drive
a car through. Not that he had the kind of enemies that
his big brother did, but in this part of town while working on the wrong end of insurance cases—you could
never be too careful.

Johnny pushed away from his desk and said, "Excuse
me, but is there a problem here?"

She looked at him as if he shouldn't have been there
or that he'd just popped in out of thin air.

"Yes!" she exclaimed. "There's a problem here! If
you've got a gun, you better get it. They're right behind
me!"

Of course, Johnny had a gun. Again, who he really was
and the high-powered friends he had in Washington made
getting the concealed-carry permit ridiculously easy.

He was about to ask exactly who *they* were, but the
mysterious young woman had already dodged into the
storage-filing room. He heard her unlatching the five
locks on the back door. Johnny stood to follow her, but
the deep-throated sound of an exhaust overlaid with ul-
traloud bass accompaniment from a car's sound system
sent him to the front door instead. Through the glass
door he saw an old Ford Fairlane convertible that was
primered, puttied and sanded beyond the point of being

able to identify an original paint color. The car was jerking up and down on the wheelbase due to some gangbanger fad modification involving hydraulics and lift-kits. That inhuman sound system was making the sides of the car visibly thump.

The five occupants of the vehicle were black, all wearing red do-rags. Two of them looked as if they'd spent time in prison and sported barely visible tattoos all over their arms and neck. The driver looked like an advertisement for Mr. T starter kits. All those gold chains had to be exhausting to wear, Johnny thought, especially considering this skinny little bastard's birdlike frame. They were all wearing the same black gangsta wraparound shades to hide the murder in their eyes, and as the car rumbled into the parking lot, the guns started to appear as if by magic.

The hoods were packing TEC-9s and 9 mm Glock pistols. Johnny didn't figure on any of these punks being world-class marksmen. But he had seen enough. He retreated into the storage room and pulled open the filing cabinet marked "Insurance." Inside the drawer were several military CS grenades. Johnny had been in the habit of packing them since the L.A. riots in the event that something similar broke out in San Diego. These jewels were extremely useful when it came to parting angry mobs. He grabbed one of the OD green canisters, pulled the pin but didn't let the spoon fly just yet. He heard the gangbangers hit the front door and go no farther. Then came the yelling and cussing punctuated by several gunshots and the crashing of glass. Johnny let the spoon fly and rolled the little surprise into his office as he pivoted and went out the back door, locking it behind him.

The CS would levitate the fight right out of those

gangbangers for longer than it took Johnny to make his escape. He still hadn't pulled his weapon from the shoulder holster underneath his blazer. There was no need for such theatrics. The threat was being neutralized without having to resort to gunfire.

Johnny calmly entered the alley behind his office and looked for the woman. She was running to the south in her stocking feet, dodging rotting refuse and clutching her shoes like family heirlooms. He whistled to get her attention. She threw a panicked glance over her shoulder, expecting to see the goon squad right behind her.

"Back this way, okay?" Johnny called after her. "You're safe now. Come on back. I'll help you."

She stopped running but still seemed hesitant.

"My car's around front."

"Oh, great! Those killers are out front, too!"

"Okay. Wait there, hide if you like. I'll get my car and pick you up. How's that?"

"If you're not back in two minutes, I'm hauling!"

"Fine. I'll be back in less than a minute. Okay?"

She nodded and ducked behind a Dumpster garbage bin. Johnny walked around the side of the building and paused at the corner. He could smell the CS now, and could hear the heaving guts and uncontrollable coughing fits of the five punks as they spilled out of the office in a white cloud of tear gas. Johnny came around the corner as the first three out ran blindly into the grille of their parked car, bounced back and plowed into the two stragglers staggering out of the office behind them. The five went down in a tangle, and they dropped their weapons as they clawed at their eyes and throats.

Johnny calmly walked into the parking lot, giving the

gangsters and the drifting CS a wide berth. He pulled his keys out of his pocket, opened the driver's door of his Saturn sedan and slid behind the wheel. He started the car, shifted into reverse and backed out in a horseshoe arch so the front of his car was now facing the white cloud that masked the front door of his office. He drove into the alley and turned left. He stopped next to the garbage bin the woman was cowering behind and unlocked the passenger door. She ran around the front of the vehicle and practically catapulted herself into the seat.

"Please, just get me out of here! Fast!"

Johnny obliged and accelerated down the alley, slowing at the mouth to look both ways before signaling and merging into traffic. He pulled his cell phone off his belt, dialed through his saved numbers until Beverly Weaver's cell number was displayed and hit Send.

Weaver was a friend of his at the San Diego Police Department. She was a member of the gang unit. She and Johnny both shared a lot of compassion for the kids on the street and worked together to help them out of the gang lifestyle.

The lady cop answered on the first ring.

"Hey, John! It's been a while. I was wondering if you were ever going to call again."

"Hey, Bev. Listen. I need you to call for backups and converge on my office. Five Blood-looking hitters just tried to pull a kidnapping or murder—I'm not sure which yet—on a new client of mine. You'll find them rolling around in the parking lot puking their guts out. They should be pretty easy to take into custody."

"What did you do to them?"

"Military CS grenade. Very effective."

Weaver laughed heartily. "Okay, I'm on it. Anything else?"

"Yeah, could you do something to secure my office? They shot out the glass and I don't want looters messing with my stuff. It's bad enough that everything's fouled with CS now."

"You got it, sugar. Thanks for the heads-up. You going to be back around to file a report?"

"Yeah. But later. I've got to get my client somewhere safe."

Through the phone, he heard Weaver hit the sirens. "I'll call you later, Johnny."

"Play smart," he said and hit the end button.

He tossed the phone on the dash and glanced over at his passenger while keeping an eye on traffic.

"I don't know if you noticed earlier but my name is John Gray."

She made a feeble attempt at a smile. "Hi. And thanks. Thanks for helping me out, a complete stranger and all."

"Well, we're not exactly total strangers anymore, are we?"

"No, I guess not."

"So what should I call you?"

"I'm Jazz. Jazz Mercedes."

"Really? That's a very unique name. You must have had interesting parents."

"My parents didn't give me my name. I did. It's my stage name."

"Are you an actress?"

"No, a dancer. I work at the Matrix."

Johnny was familiar with the place. He'd been in

once or twice on business. It was a strip bar that catered to the middle-class professional man.

"How long have you been doing that?"

"Since I was seventeen."

"Uh-huh. Do the owners know they hired an underage dancer?"

"Nope. I have a real good fake ID. I've got friends that make them on their computers."

"I've got friends like that."

"I'm sorry, Johnny, but what did you say you do again?"

"I didn't say. I'm a private investigator."

"Sounds kind of exotic."

"It is on TV. In real life, it's really pretty pedestrian. Today was the exception to the rule."

"I take it damsels in distress don't crash your office every day being chased by gun-toting criminals."

"It's never happened. Until today."

"Must be your lucky day."

"Must be."

"It must be *my* lucky day. It must be fate. Do you believe in fate?"

"More than you will know," he said. And he winked at her with those ghostly blue eyes.

"IT'S ME," was all Mack Bolan said. The man known as the Executioner was talking on a pay phone outside the rest rooms in a Denny's restaurant off the freeway.

"Hey, Sarge. It's damn good to hear your voice again. We need to stay in touch more."

"Same here, Leo. It's been too damn long."

"Where are you, Sarge?"

"Arlington. I'm in a Denny's using the phone to call you back."

"Hey, do you think you could make it out here tonight? You don't have anything more pressing, do you?"

"Actually, I'm just enjoying a little downtime. What's up, Leo?"

"I'd rather not go into details on an unsecured line. Know what I mean?"

Bolan chuckled. "I'm on my way. It's really good to talk to you again, guy."

"Hey, stop it. I'm getting all choked up."

"Sure you are. Talk to you in a few."

"I'm waiting."

Bolan hung up the phone.

BOLAN TWISTED the cap off the bottle of beer Leo Turrin had offered him and took a long pull. He didn't often find an excuse to drink, but tonight was a good one. Old friends reunited. Leo looked good. It was hard to believe that at one time the Executioner had actually tried to kill him. It seemed like ages now since Bolan had discovered that the man who had pimped the Executioner's sister was actually an undercover federal agent working to bring down the Pittsfield Mafia. Bolan realized that Turrin was fighting the same war as he was, but with different rules of engagement. He couldn't fault the Fed for that.

"What have you got, Leo?"

Turrin frowned, took a pull of his own beer and mulled over his words before speaking.

"I was tailed and approached today by a crew of wise guys. Three of them."

Bolan sat forward, all ears now, his eyes narrowing with concern.

"They didn't—"

"No, no," Turrin said quickly, waving off the thought

that was occurring to Bolan. "They weren't there to whack me. They wanted me to come out of retirement."

"What? Why?"

"They need somebody to put a very special kind of crew together for them. The guy who approached me is an intermediary for an offshore interest, was how he put it. I've been checking out this guy's story and references all night long, and he checks out perfectly."

The morning's newspaper was neatly piled on the table next to Turrin. He reached under the paper, pulled out a manila file folder and slid it across the tabletop. Bolan opened the file, which wasn't very thick. It contained about twenty or thirty pages of printouts off the Internet. The top page was a printout from the story archives of *The New York Times*. The headline read: JEFFERSON MANHATTAN OIL OFFSHORE PROJECT ABANDONED. Bolan's eyes widened at the reference to the oil company.

The patriarch of Jefferson Manhattan Oil Company and its subsidiary, Jefferson Manhattan Banks, was none other than Mason Jefferson. Jefferson was one of the thirteen "brain cells" behind a conspiracy Mack Bolan had recently shut down in a command strike that started outside Midland, Texas, and spilled over into the supersecret Area 51 in Nevada.

"It's incredible the information you can access now off the Internet," Turrin said. "Everything in that file came from public sources. I didn't use any of my government clout at all."

Bolan grunted an affirmative. He was too engrossed in the news item to offer anything more intelligible than that.

Dateline: the North Atlantic, thirty-one miles north-northwest of Bermuda. Promising recon drillings have located a substantial oil field in twelve hundred feet of water. The Jefferson Manhattan Oil Company secured drilling rights to the area and has immediately launched into construction operations to plant a deep-sea drilling platform directly above the find. The skyscraper-high prefab support columns were transported to the site by barge and dropped into the ocean. Simultaneously, construction of the steel skeletons of the above-water decks started while diving crews began work on securing the support pylons into the ocean bed on gigantic caissons. But divers began to disappear. After an underwater diver's habitat was "attacked" and destroyed under mysterious circumstances, nobody would sign on to complete the work at any price. Rumors of the Bermuda Triangle and sea monsters are rife. With cost overruns mounting into the tens of millions, Jefferson Manhattan Oil decided to cut its losses before a serious financial disaster sent shock waves through the entire Jefferson mineral-banking conglomerate. The project was abandoned. The mystery of the disappearance continues. The partially completed offshore platform has remained abandoned in the middle of the hostile ocean for more than a decade.

Bolan looked up at Turrin after finishing the news item, but didn't offer a comment.

The next piece showed a picture of a man with the eyes of a hawk and the face of a fallen angel. His features were a study in severe sincerity. His eyes were dark enough to make the irises almost invisible. His neck was a stump that his head seemed an extension of.

His name was Damien Cassandra, and he was now the owner of the ghost platform. The next part of the story took a turn for the unexpected. Cassandra transformed the abandoned platform into an officially recognized "nation" in the eyes of the United Nations General Assembly and even had an ambassador to the UN on behalf of this artificial country. Cassandra had dubbed this new man-made island state "Cassiopeia" after the Greek goddess. As a nation, Cassiopeia was being set up to have the highest GNP of any country on earth. The "republic" of Cassiopeia was into the business of exporting high-octane party materials: the best methamphetamine on the planet, made with a new revolutionary manufacturing method.

Bolan skimmed the rest of the article and noted the detailed diagrams mapping the environmental "sandwich" built six decks down from the original level one superstructure of the offshore platform.

"It's disturbing," Bolan said. "I haven't heard a damned thing about this until now."

Turrin nodded. "Read on. There's more that hasn't been aired in this country, and I have a reason and a culprit as to why."

Next in line was a news story filed that morning. The article sketched out the meager details of an incident on the Cassiopeia platform that forced the emergency evacuation of visitors and citizens alike. Many were feared missing and dead. An extensive floating marina was built around the platform to accommodate the rush of party-hungry visitors that immediately began visiting the platform when the "nation" had officially opened her doors to the world on the first of January. The crush of private boats overwhelmed the available berthing spaces.

Some time after midnight, the flotilla around Cassiopeia was destroyed by an unknown force in the ocean. Every vessel was crushed and sunk. The passengers of the vessels were thrown into the churning waters and dragged down to their deaths. Eyewitness accounts told of horrifying serpentlike monsters attacking with no more warning than the choking smell of ammonia right before the attack commenced. Four known survivors were airlifted to the King Edward VII Memorial Hospital in Bermuda. Whatever was lurking in the depths was probably still there, and until the internal security forces could determine the cause and destroy it, Cassiopeia was off-limits to all comers.

All international offers of help were being refused. Cassiopeia had "other options" in that respect.

The American media was strangely silent on the story. None of the networks and none of the dailies were picking up the story at all. Apparently, the solution to the Bermuda Triangle mystery just wasn't considered news in the United States.

Bolan set the folder aside and looked at Turrin.

"Okay, Leo. Why isn't this story being covered here? This is a huge news story."

"It has to do with the silent partnership that has made this little experiment in nation-building a reality."

"Talk to me, Leo."

"Our man Cassandra has huge support from the Outfit. They're heavily invested. That's what my surprise suitor had to reveal. But the Outfit is in alliance with Langley as well."

"The Company is sponsoring this?"

Turrin nodded. "It's all about funding black ops off the books."

Bolan chewed on that. He had no real love for the CIA. It had gotten in the way of Stony Man operations on more than one occasion. He often wondered who really set the tone for American foreign policy: the office of the President or the office of the director of Central Intelligence. Bolan was inclined to believe that the President was fast becoming a figurehead for the real powers that be in Wonderland.

The Executioner was very uncomfortable with that thought.

"What exactly do the wise guys want you to assemble for them?" he asked.

"Hunters with no fear and a love of money. And some experts."

"What kind of experts?"

"Marine biology experts. Scientific advisers."

"All right. I want you to assemble some torpedoes, call in some favors and make it happen. I'll handle the experts. How long do we have to get this thing going?"

"Forty-eight hours."

"Okay. Let's make it happen, Leo."

3

Coastal Swamps near Savannah, Georgia

Special Agent Mallory Harmon was convinced that they were going to feed her to the alligators. After they were done with her. That's how the bodies were being disposed of. She was sure of it now because she'd captured one of the big bull bastards two nights ago with the help of two sympathetic members of the Parks Service. The seven-foot male gator was darted and whisked to a veterinary hospital in Savannah, where Dr. Lynzie Strauss performed an exploratory surgery on the reptile's stomach and bowels. That prehistoric throwback was gorged on human meat and body parts. Once the evidence was found, the alligator was sewn back up and taken into custody as a key witness in the case Harmon was building against the Rasmussin clan.

Ever since her brief but very interesting attachment to what FBI official records and memoranda would only refer to as STF Zulu or Special Task Force Zulu, Harmon, an agent who was also a medical doctor, had discovered a much higher tolerance within the command structure of the FBI for her private crusades. Her special interests that were way outside the norms for internal FBI culture. Hobbies that were jokingly called "monster hunts" behind the petite but brilliant agent's back.

Harmon was wondering just how she was going to get out of her current situation.

Her hands were tied behind her back, and they had put a ball gag in her mouth. She had been stripped to her bra and panties. The gang hadn't raped her—yet. She knew that would be coming. They would rape her and torture her and mutilate her until she died, then they'd feast on her heart and burn her intestines— yanked from her belly and heaped into a bloody pile on what amounted to an oversized incense burner and set ablaze in honor of some horrible deity lost in antiquity.

Special Agent Mallory Harmon of the FBI's Behavioral Sciences Unit had a pretty in-depth understanding of what this ordeal would entail before the sweet release of death was granted.

These were the ritual characteristics of some of the most brutal crimes that the National Crime Computer had on record, and they had been growing in frequency over the past ten years. Since the approach of the millennium. Her sideline tracking of these incidents over time and geography had pinpointed some interesting characteristics shared by all the data. She had read that when bodies were found, the corpses were always located in a subterranean crime scene or were found near a very sizable body of water. A lake or swamp or an ocean. More than seventy-five percent of the time, the ritual victim was found located in view of the water.

Something about the water was very important to these perps. The perps themselves, when caught, were varied in occupation and station in life. That was the strangest thing about this phenomenon she was tracking. Its vertical distribution through society at large. From lone individuals to groups of people, from inbred Louisiana swamp dwellers to the highest ranks of privilege. Every perp showed exactly the same beliefs that were motivating exactly the same kinds of crimes. But between the killers or groups of killers, there was never any formal link. None of those captured and interviewed ever had an idea that there were others just like them. Even the groups echoed this same belief. In their eyes, the group was a singular entity. They had no idea that there were other groups in the world of very parallel beliefs and ritual activity.

Harmon was keen to these distinctions. She had written a special program that watched the data being added daily to the National Crime Computer and downloaded crimes to the computer in her office that fit these very exacting parameters. When a file came up, she labeled it a Special Interest file and gave it a number on a master sheet. More often than not, she found a way to get sent into the area to investigate, to aid local law enforcement in profiling the perp or perps. The resulting field reports from Special Agent Harmon were always the source of great alarm among her superiors.

A week ago the file had showed up in her downloads. A runaway teenager named Bruce Baxter was found on a desolate beach near Savannah. The discovery indicated the kind of cult activity that she was trying to pinpoint, study up close and then somehow neutralize. It was the first such incident in the area. Whether this fact indicated that a loner had recently wandered into the area had yet to be determined.

Today, this second, Mallory Harmon knew exactly what category to place Baxter's ritual murder in.

It was a group effort here tonight outside Savannah, Georgia. All of them were going to take some kind of poke at her…even the degenerate female members of the inbred family clan-cult. She was on display before the assembled faithful on top of a dais like an artifact at an auction. At this auction, everyone would get a piece of the piece on the auction block. The dais was like a small stage she shared with the stone altar to lay her body on and the incense burner for her guts. The bowl that would be the funeral pyre of her intestines was carved out of basaltic rock.

A small wooden foldout table was at the head of the altar that her clothes, gun and cell phone were arranged on. Her backup plan wasn't operating like a well-oiled machine. She was wondering if maybe her backup had decided to go to the tittie bar instead. She was scared, and she couldn't help but show the fear in her eyes, but her mind was still running angles and looking for anything that could be used as an opening to make a move.

If she could only get to the gun, the cell phone…

She eyed the cavernous interior of the barn in the flickering of candles and torchlight. It would be a flat-out thirty-yard dash to the barn doors. She'd have to run right through the dancing dervish ranks of the thirteen Rasmussins, three of whom were female and had all borne children for the ten men. They were all cousins and brothers and sisters, mixing and mixing again, each generation genetically degenerating more frighteningly than the last.

While each of the members of the Rasmussin clan could easily pass themselves off as a "normal" human being inside a crowd, the group seemed to share certain abnormal characteristics. Long teeth, especially the canines. Lank and elongated limbs, hunched postures—a couple of the older ones were genuine hunchbacks. Their eyes were all the same vivid color of green, their cheekbones were high and they all had raven-black hair.

Their robes were crude handmade productions that lacked the polish of a costuming department. The sacred color scheme of the robe was purple, royal blue and black. The analytical part of her mind made a note about the colors. To be chosen as the colors of their ritual garments, the three hues had to have a very important symbolic significance inside their religion. On the left breast of each garment was a similar octopus-like beast with eyes like blood splatters.

The octopus motif was another universal that cropped up a lot in these cases. Often the bodies were being found with such a figure carved or tattooed on the victim's chest. The creature was important. It had to represent their god. It was the closest living thing on Earth to what represented their deity's most striking characteristics.

Harmon was amazed by her own mind in this crisis. She was crazy with fear and anxiety and yet, somewhere above all that, she was playing social anthropologist, making checklists for a research paper.

A third area of her mind was screaming: *Why isn't somebody wondering what's become of me?*

The senior Rasmussin looked more like a werewolf than any of the rest of the clan. He had thick coarse black hair on his shoulders, chest and back. With the beard and lupine features, Harmon thought he was one scary dude to have leering at her with bloodlust in his eyes, a butcher knife in his hand and a hard-on like carved teak. He was stalking around her on the dais, chanting in some dialect that she didn't recognize.

Another wave of fear flashed through her mind.

Mallory Harmon had to assume that she was on her own.

The cavalry wasn't going to get her out of this one.

SAC BRAD FENDER DROVE into the assembly area with his lights off. Black figures milled around in the dark, moving between the three vans parked in the picnic area off the county hard-pack road. A big coffee dispenser was set up on one of the picnic tables, and the FBI's equivalent to a SWAT team took turns refilling mugs and playing laser tag with one another with their night vision and laser targeting devices.

Fender left his sedan idling while he got out of the car and began asking the closest black wraiths about who exactly was in charge. When he finally located the squad leader, he asked, "Where's Agent Harmon?"

The squad leader's equipment shifted as the man shrugged in the darkness.

"Downrange, I guess."

"Do you know if she's all right? Has she checked in?"

"I've got guys watching the objective. Last I heard it's all quiet."

"I don't believe this."

"Hey, if she gets her panties in a pinch, all she has to do is make a phone call."

"What if she's been relieved of her ability to make that call? Did you think about that?"

The sound of shrugging again. "I'm just doing what I've been told."

"Okay. I've been told by the director himself to produce Agent Harmon immediately. That means alive and well and in one piece. Now, where is she?"

"Downrange snooping around that alligator farm for vampires or some shit."

"How long's she been out of contact?"

"A couple hours maybe."

"Goddammit! And that doesn't concern you?"

"Hey, she's a nutcase! Everyone knows it!"

"She's an agent of the FBI, like you and me. If she's dead or in trouble out there because you don't care about a fellow agent with strange ideas, I'm going to hang every one of you bastards, and the director's going to have to wait in line to get a piece of your ass! Now get these men ready to move in!

"Now!" Fender yelled.

THE BARN DOOR opened with a creak, and a clansman poked his head through the crack.

"Lights!" he hissed. "Cars coming!"

The clan went into action. The revelers on the packed dirt floor ran to the walls of the barn on each side and exchanged butchering sickles for rifles and shotguns that were on hand for just such an emergency. Whatever these kinfolk were losing of the higher language functions through interbreeding, they had more than made up for in sheer animal reflexes.

The senior Rasmussin, Jimbo Raz as he was called by business associates from the seamier side of Savannah, whirled away from staring down Harmon and rasped, "Gator bait them all!"

The disciples made a rush for the doors.

The cell phone and pager both went off within a nanosecond of the other, chirping and trilling for attention, too. Chaos was crashing the party in all the wrong places, and Harmon forgot about fear and observations.

She seized her opening.

"TURN THOSE damn lights out!" the HRT leader yelled over the radio.

Fender grabbed the mike off the dash and replied, "Everybody hit your lights and flashers! I just called Agent Harmon's cell and pager! Everybody listen for a phone ringing and move in on it!"

"That's your plan?"

"You got a better one?"

"Yeah, we could have gone in dark!"

"I'm calling the shots now! Shut up and follow me in!"

Fender wheeled off the county road and through the gate. A sign flashed by on the left: The Raz-Muh-Taz Gator Farms. In bad hand lettering underneath the title it said *Been open long time now.* It was a phrase calculated to put the consumer at ease.

HARMON DROPPED to a crouch and slipped her bound wrists under her nylon-slick rump like a seat. She dropped to the dais onto her shoulders and did a back roll while tucking her feet and knees through the cradle of her arms, then jumped to her feet again. Her bound hands were now in front. She leaped forward and jumped into the air, drop-kicking Jimbo Raz heels-to-kidney. Jimbo was catapulted off the dais and into the dirt face first. Harmon hit the rough wood planking and rolled into the little table, toppling it. She scrambled to grab the Glock with her tied hands.

Her bound wrists actually facilitated taking up a natural two-handed weapon grip. She flicked off the safety with the thumb of her firing hand and sat up, bringing the pistol on target as Jimbo seemed to levitate to his feet. He turned and leaped at her.

She fired two rounds on blind instinct.

Her instincts were good. The top of Jimbo's head from the uni-brow up blew apart into frothy chunks of skull and bleeding brain tissue. The psycho aberration was dead before his body kissed the dirt.

FENDER SKIDDED across loose gravel in a clearing that served as a parking lot. He rammed the transmission into Park and kicked the door open as he hauled out the bullhorn. None of the HRT vehicles had heeded the order to go in lit up like Christmas trees.

He didn't even have the time to yell something impressive into the compound before two shots echoed and the tac-net came to life with a cross-crackle of radio reports and rapid-fire commands.

"Shots fired! Shots fired!"

"All stations! Weapons free! I repeat—weapons free! Engage all hostiles and neutralize!"

Fender keyed the bullhorn and boomed, "This is the FBI! You're surrounded!"

The globes of flash from muzzle-blasts in the shadows around the barn and main house came back like one unified voice. The kinfolk didn't recognize the FBI's jurisdiction here.

Red laser dots were dancing all over on tree trunks and wood siding on the enemy's side of the skirmish. The HRT shock troops returned fire in controlled bursts and only when the individual soldier was positively locked on to a legitimate target. When the kinfolk returned fire, there were fewer muzzle-flashes involved in the salvo.

A couple or three more exchanges like that and the

resistance would be down for the count, dead or begging for triage.

TWO OF THE THREE women in the pack attacked Harmon like velociraptors, hitting her from the front and rear simultaneously. Both of her feral attackers were armed with oak staves tipped with eight-inch Bowie knives. Harmon dived and rolled as the woman to the rear threw everything she had into a kidney stab. The intended target was no longer there, but the assassin's buddy was.

The female charging Harmon's front took the rear attacker's knife through the solar plexus, and the blade exploded out her back in a blood gruel spray. Harmon twisted out of the roll and shot the final marauder in the back of the head.

Harmon got to her knees and scrambled over to the body of the impaled female. She mounted the dying woman and used the gore-lubed blade jutting out of the downed attacker's spine to cut the twine binding her wrists. With her hands free, she was ready for all takers now.

IF HE COULD HAVE been seen clearly in the light, the PVS-7 monocle NVD goggles mounted in front of his eyes would have made him look like a Borg cyclops. In the gray-green resolution of the goggles, he saw the white-hot dot of the laser on the target's chest. The target looked like something out of *The Howling*—bipedal and feral but toting a Remington bolt-action rifle. He was squeezing the trigger when the target was capped from behind, and a glassy bulb of light expanded then shattered into afterimage marking the muzzle-blast of the killing round. The HRT shooter directed his attention there, and a tawny ghost of emerald-shaded marble padded out of the barn on bare feet, wearing only a bra and panties. She blew out another target's spine before the shooter could make the call to the net.

"Check fire! Check fire! We have a friendly in the open! I think it's Agent Harmon."

THE RASMUSSIN kinfolk were put down in the time-honored tradition of Old Yeller: a bullet to the brainpan. There wasn't a cure for their kind of rabies. Agent Harmon, still wearing nothing but her undies, directed the sealing of the crime scene and made sure that all the weird occult paraphernalia in the house and in the barn be tagged, bagged and loaded into her sedan. For many of the FBI men there that night, it was the first time they'd become aware that Special Agent Harmon was actually a woman as well. A damned attractive one, too. It was the first time that she was looked at as something other than a crackpot and the laughingstock of the FBI. Special Agent in Charge Fender couldn't get a word in edgewise; the sight of her like that was just crashing his speech centers.

Fender got it together enough to start following her around while she went to find the HRT commander.

Her bra was forest-green and her panties were red bikinis, but she didn't look like a Christmas present with her disheveled hair, sweaty sheen and Glock pistol clutched in a tight fist at her side. Her gunslinger stance seemed very incongruent with her appearance.

"So what finally gave it away that I could use some of that backup you were jealously withholding?" she asked him.

The HRT commander answered on the defensive. "I didn't withhold anything. You said you were going to signal us for help."

"You didn't get my signal?"

"No. What was it?"

She answered his question with a knee snapped into the man's groin with everything she could put into it.

"That was the signal. Do you get the goddamn signal now?"

She left the HRT commander in the dirt and started to head back to the barn. Fender didn't do anything about the assault on a federal agent he'd just witnessed. If it had been him, he'd have done the same thing.

"You look like you're trying to tell me something, Fender."

"Yeah. The director sent me out to bring you in."

"Bring me in? That doesn't sound good, Fender. Am I a fugitive now?"

"No, just reassigned. Some special task force called Zulu."

Harmon stopped in her tracks. "I'm back on Zulu?"

"Yeah. What is that?"

"Fender, I know this sounds clichéd, but if I told you, I really would have to kill you. I've got to get dressed and get the hell out of here."

She started to run off to get her clothes but remembered something and spun back to face the SAC.

"Oh yeah. Where am I going and who do I report to?"

"You're going to Arkham, Massachusetts, and once there you will activate a Dr. West at Miskatonic University. He's doing a series of lectures there."

"They don't need him." Mallory Harmon groused. "Why do they bother with him?"

She didn't expect any kind of an answer from the man. She pivoted on the balls of her bare feet and ran with a newfound purpose toward the barn. Many of her fellow agents' eyes followed her until she was out of view. Brad Fender found himself replaying a line from a Jethro Tull song; something about watching the pretty panties run.

Mallory Harmon was earning a whole new reputation now among the field personnel of the Federal Bureau of Investigation.

It was now going to be said that not only was she a kook, but that she looked absolutely fantastic running and shooting bad guys wearing nothing but her undies.

Mallory Harmon had finally and irrevocably been noticed.

4

Miskatonic University, Arkham, Massachusetts

"Dr. West?"

Donovan West looked up from his lecture notes. He was becoming the Wade Cook of scientific seminars, beginning to earn both a handsome living and an even better reputation in his newfound field of expertise: nanotechnology. His astounding insights into this fledgling area of technical know-how were hardly the result of original research. His observations and suggestions were the result of long hours logged in his own private lab studying the nano-mechanisms he'd extracted from the world's first known metahuman, the person who had been conditioned to call himself Splatterpunk. Nano-realities were still fogging his brain when he looked up, and he had to blink several times to tighten up his focus on the world outside of his head.

A graduate student, a very pretty one, was standing in front of the desk wearing a heavy sweater dress, black tights and mukluks. The chill of winter still had hold of most mornings until noon. The young woman had a backpack full of textbooks over one shoulder, and she held a small brown wrapped box in her hand.

"I was told to give this to you. It's supposed to be important."

West took the package. "Yes, yes. Thank you."

The young woman was relieved to be off the hook and quickly retreated out of his borrowed office. West tore the brown wrap off the box and opened it. Inside was a standard microcassette recorder. Intrigued by this unorthodox approach, he pushed the play button.

He didn't know what to expect, but what he got was absolutely the last thing he would have expected.

It was *her* voice.

"Hello, West."

The recorded female voice was dripping with sarcasm. "I'm waiting for you out front in the silver Crown Victoria with U.S. government plates. Come along peacefully, West. I'm authorized to arrest you if you refuse my invitation."

The tape hissed for a heartbeat.

"It's Zulu, West. They need us again."

Donovan West blanched, his heart skipped a beat in excitement and he quickly shoved his lecture notes into a battered brown leather bag. He walked out of the office and completely forgot about telling anyone at the university that he was leaving and how long he might be gone.

All he heard was her voice ringing in his ear.

"It's Zulu, West."

THE ROOM WAS antiseptic white and polished to an inspection-ready shine. There were no windows in any of the four walls, and there was no clock. A white marker board the size of a schoolroom chalkboard was fastened to the wall at the front of the room, but nothing was written on it. The room was much longer than it was wide.

Two rows of seven chairs sat against two sides of the room with a narrow center aisle up the middle. A windowless door was in the wall to the right of the marker board. A skinny white podium stood at the front of the room for the debriefing officer.

The debriefing officer was an older lady who had said that her name was Martha Hibbins, but Mallory Harmon was convinced it was false. The two of them were inside the "Puzzle Palace" now.

Agent Harmon and Dr. West were beginning to feel like mushrooms.

The two of them were filling out the power of attorney forms that were included inside their contracting packets, and Martha was insisting on doing these things by the block number. No skipping ahead. Everyone stayed together, and it was done at *her* pace. Harmon had personally seen pond water move faster than this. She and West were being called upon to serve on a supersecret task force where time was probably a key factor in the success matrix of the operation, and yet the paperwork had to be done to the letter.

The two of them had been through three forms now, but it seemed like nine hundred at the debriefing officer's pace.

Harmon and West exchanged painful glances across the narrow center aisle. It was going to be a long day.

HARMON AND WEST had no idea that they were looking at a genuine Stony Man Farm internal security blacksuit. For that matter, the two contract operatives had no idea that they were working for Stony Man Farm. They had never even heard of Stony Man Farm.

The man was wearing coveralls with no name tape.

He had identified himself as Raul. The three of them were standing at the back of a white van with no rear compartment windows. The rear doors were open, revealing two padded bench seats along the inside length of the cargo area. And that was all there was to the rear compartment. Two bench seats. The cab of the van was inaccessible. A steel firewall was custom built between the two spaces.

The blacksuit in coveralls was explaining the theory of the wheels before them. "This ride is designed to baffle even the best direction-distance man or woman. Some people seem to have the ability to 'feel' distances and directions being traveled even when visual references are removed. This van is designed to dampen the vibrations that supply this kind of information to people who are very 'in tune' with their, shall we say, vehicular surroundings. Our algorithms indicate that the two of you possess less than a two percent chance of being any good at this very esoteric skill anyway."

"So why don't you just throw us in a trunk then?" Harmon asked.

The blacksuit grinned and chuckled knowingly.

"You have a 98.6 percentile chance of always confronting unknowns and perceived threats with some form of 'smart-ass comeback.' So far our bar graphs on you are DOT."

The acronym ended up having the most annoyance factor of anything he just said.

"DOT? What the hell is DOT?"

That smile again; the one that knew more than should rightly be available to strangers or government agencies.

"Dead On Target," he explained.

MALLORY HARMON didn't like being DOT. She suspected that their psychological evaluations under Martha Hibbins had more than likely taken place in or around the "District of Corruption." Her sense of time told her that the van was either in Virginia or Philly or West Virginia—if their driver had taken flight to the west. She doubted the west was a possible direction of travel. She'd had no sense of climbing since the drive had begun. The van might be slick, but had they thought about the ear popping that went along with elevation changes in their sensory dampening designs? Maybe. Maybe not.

Harmon had learned to trust what her intangibles were telling her.

The van wasn't traveling inland. It was following the coastline either north or south. Not that she was truly obsessed with knowing her location. Playing the game was something to do in transit. Once she was aware that the van was designed to beat her, she had to test it. She made her guess. Her intangibles said that she was in Virginia.

She'd go with that until proved otherwise.

West was preoccupied with notes. He put on reading glasses and went over page after page of scribbled hieroglyphics that only he could interpret. If West died of a hemorrhaged bowel at that moment, she doubted anyone on the planet could figure out what those notes said in plain English.

When the van finally stopped and the rear doors opened, Harmon was denied anything that might betray their location. The van was in a large underground garage, very much like the garage that this journey had started from. Other government vehicles were parked there. Several more vans, Crown Victoria sedans, a couple of military Hummers.

"I think we're in Virginia," Harmon told the blacksuit.

Before the guy could catch himself, he gave away just the slightest facial tic, a flinch that told Harmon her guess was goddamned DOT. They'd probably spend ten million redesigning the van now. A two-percentile had sensed through the best countermeasures money could pay to devise. That just wasn't right. It wouldn't be right until the taxpayers had a van that nobody could read the road through.

The blacksuit escorted the two of them to an elevator, put them on board and punched an unmarked button on the panel.

"It'll feel like the elevator is going up," he told Harmon. "That's because it is."

He grinned from the alcove and the door closed on his face.

The woman waiting in the alcove when the elevator doors opened was tall and blond. Harmon and West had met the striking woman on one other occasion— the last time that they'd been assigned to something that was dubbed "Zulu" in the post-operative phase. Barbara Price, once again, seemed so very…*genuine.* She wasn't another spook with a cover story to regurgitate on cue when small talk became verbal probes for background.

Price lit up at the sight of the two contract specialists to Stony Man Farm.

"Dr. West! Dr. Harmon! It's wonderful to have you back. And so soon, too."

"The world must be going to the Dog Star," Harmon said.

Price caught the sly little test of knowledge that Mallory Harmon had just zinged at her.

She didn't miss a beat with her reply. "Or Sirius is coming here."

Harmon chuckled. "Exactly my thoughts as well."

Donovan West wasn't exactly sure what the exchange between the two women had accomplished. He just kept his mouth shut. Price stepped aside to give the two contract operatives the run of the hallway and took up the rear. Harmon hugged the left side of the corridor and West stayed tight right. The two scientists didn't seem to get along very well. Price knew that it was a sign that the two really liked each other. She'd seen this syndrome many times before.

Price led them to a door with a steel-reinforced jamb. An electronic keypad was mounted in the wall to the right of the doorway. The green LCD read: Open.

On the other side of the door was a large room with a gigantic conference-style table as centerpiece, and the walls were ringed with giant monitors that were all receiving a blue screen feed.

Price indicated the seats surrounding the table. "Have a seat and I'll bring you both up to speed on what Colonel Pollock would like you to do for him."

West raised his hand while asking, "Yes, Miss Price. I'm wondering if we're still free to walk away from this arrangement as we were before?"

Harmon frowned, thinking that it was a good question coming from a second-rate source.

Price said very firmly, "Absolutely. This is strictly a volunteers-only mission."

"Thank you, Miss Price. I elect to continue this assignment. I just like to know that the door is still there."

Harmon experienced that flash of knowing something, and it felt like an irresistible itch in her aura. She had to immediately confirm her hunch.

"So, West. You must actually be reading Ian Fleming now instead of just watching the slapstick interpretation of Fleming on home videocassette."

Harmon's sudden inquiry was like being unexpectedly impaled. Donovan West flinched. It was the woman's unpredictability that razzed him the most. West was an inherently ordered man, and Harmon's chaotically indulgent and disordered approach to the world left the nanoscientist feeling assaulted in her presence.

Price deployed the two file folders stamped EYES ONLY. She handed the bottom file to Mallory Harmon and the remaining went to Donovan West. Harmon didn't wait for permission to look at the contents. She broke the paper seal and pulled out the contents. ID cards fell out as part of the total package. She looked at her new driver's license from the state of Maryland.

She raised an eyebrow. "Do I look like an Abbi with an *i* Bainbridge to you? Would it be possible for us to choose our own code names?"

"Not at this time," Price replied.

West tore the seal off his file folder and rummaged around inside until he found a piece of cover ID. He scrutinized his name and smiled.

"James W. Solo. At your service."

"All right," Price groused. "The ad-lib version of this briefing, then. Now that you have both acquainted yourselves with your covers, let me add that you're both supposed to be experts in marine biology as well. Since the two of you are very intelligent, we didn't think that this cover would be too much of a stretch for either of you. You'll both be playing scientists—just two scientists who happen to be experts in marine biology."

Harmon was reading ahead. She briefly studied the spy satellite photo of the Cassiopeia platform and read the situation data. Her brow furrowed. "This offshore rig is experiencing trouble with an unknown and hostile marine life-form? Is that correct?"

Price nodded. "Yes, that's the story as we understand it right now."

Harmon was skimming for clues. There. She read them off for West's benefit. "A creature or creatures. Described consistently by witnesses as looking like snakes or serpents. The appearance of the creature or creatures coincides with a choking smell of ammonia. The creature or creatures twists and bites its victims to pieces. Leaves ringed bruises on bodies that were recovered."

She looked up from the file. "I can tell you what this thing is. Its scientific name is *Architeuthis dux*. All that science knows of these animals is from the few dead carcasses that have washed ashore in the past century. Science has never observed *Architeuthis* before alive in the wild. From the looks of this brief, I'd say that there is more than one animal out there. There are probably dozens of them. Some of the specimens have to be absolutely huge if they're sinking ninety- and one hundred-foot yachts. I hope that we haven't been brought in on this just to identify the creatures."

"No, Dr. Harmon, you have more of an active role in this mission than just IDing some of the culprits."

West was struggling with the beast's name. *"Archi-teuthis...Architeuthis?"*

Harmon threw out the giveaway clue. "Ever see *Twenty Thousand Leagues Beneath the Sea?* Remember that big thing with tentacles that attacked the submarine near the end of the movie?"

"Yes! Of course! The giant squid!"

"Bingo."

5

The Cassiopeia Platform

The sky was formless and gray. There had been no sunrise, just a steady diffusion from darkness to light. The horizon in all directions had the feel of being stillborn, incomplete. A finely misted rain created a curtain that surrounded the concrete-and-steel island in the middle of the Atlantic. The ocean below was agitated, swirling and swelling, rising and falling off, a cold blue topography in constant flux.

Bolan, Harmon and West were the only passengers on the refurbished Huey. The cabin doors were closed, and the interior of the helicopter was soundproofed and outfitted like an airline shuttle, not a bird of war. It was a VIP bird in the Cassiopeia air force. Their Air Force One.

Jack Grimaldi had airlifted the Stony Man team to La Guardia International Airport where they boarded a commercial flight to Bermuda. The team was met in Bermuda by a representative from the offshore nation and assigned to a helicopter for the hop out to the platform.

With the prevailing weather, the bird was nearly right on top of the platform before the squat titan of concrete and steel was fully revealed through the rain fog. Bolan was expecting something that looked more like an oil rig. The overhead satellite image didn't give a lot of information about the structure in a profile view. Drawings and pictures taken from miles above didn't do justice to this feat of crazy engineering erected in the middle of the North Atlantic. By all rights, man had no business establishing beachheads in the middle of Nature this raw.

The helicopter was approaching the platform from a northern flight path, toward the south face of Cassiopeia. As an oil rig being born, the offshore platform had developed as far as dropping the five prefab support columns into the water and constructing the first level of the actual platform, sitting like a steel tabletop on huge concrete legs. It was at this stage that the Jefferson Manhattan Oil Company abandoned construction.

When the Cassiopeia Trust of Companies acquired the deed to the offshore platform, the steel superstructure of the above-water deck was showing the signs of severe deterioration. The giant concrete support cylinders that anchored the platform to the sea floor were the only original construction that was preserved. The first deck of the platform was rebuilt and surfaced with concrete slabs. A hurricane-worthy maintenance hangar was built on the huge tabletop to maintain the fleet of Hueys. Two more hangars were built adjacent to the maintenance shelter. These would house Cassiopeia's aircraft during periods of bad weather.

Citizens and employees alike referred to this level as the hangar deck. It was the anchor point for the "environmental sandwich" that was built beneath the deck and constructed like an inverted pyramid. Each of the six levels was a little smaller than the one above so the structure staircased toward the ocean like a big wide V. The last level of the structure was only forty feet above the surface of the Atlantic. As things were standing now, that was way too close to the water. Level Six was called the observation lounge before it became the LP-OP— listening post-observation post—for a command and control element that was probably coordinating from one of the big hangars. The observation lounge was surrounded on all sides by a redwood deck, polymer sealed to combat the effects of seawater, which almost doubled the floor space of the indoor lounge. Descending from the deck on four sides was an angled staircase with two landings. The stairs connected the party palace above to the floating marina below.

The marina was a floating wastewater of debris from what had to have been several hundred pleasure craft. The mind was completely boggled at the level of violence and destruction that was evidenced by the scene below.

Mack Bolan could hardly believe his eyes.

The floating hull fragments were a jigsaw puzzle of makes, models and economic status. There were dozens of bigger vessels all but submerged and left relatively intact. Harmon was swearing up and down that the creatures were, in fact, the rarest and, some felt, most vicious predators to ever inhabit the ocean. Certainly the question over the animals' vicious distemper was now an answered one.

The thought of the waters below being filled with maybe hundreds of those beasts, a battalion-sized element of giant squid hovering in wait of the next feeding, was so far outside Bolan's usual mission parameters to be almost surreal. But the specter of the squid wasn't the focus of the mission. The platform itself and the nature of its backing were the pieces of key intelligence that needed to be confirmed. If Bolan confirmed Leo's intel, the Executioner was going to sink Cassiopeia like a big rock.

It wasn't the drugs that Mack Bolan was so hot to shut down. He was realistic enough to know that human beings had been getting high and getting drunk since history had been in motion. It was the fact that cannibals were in the driver's seat on this subject and making big bank to further the feeding frenzy of a pack of predators turned loose on the world at large. If it had been ball bearings instead of cocaine or methamphetamine, it would have made no difference. If the cannibals were getting fat from trafficking in something, Bolan was sure to find a way to throw a speed bump in all that traffic. It went back to simple infantry tactics. An enemy had to have a supply line to prosper and survive. If the supply line was cut the enemy would eventually wither away and die.

It was pure tactics.

Bolan wasn't fighting his war born of morality.

It was all tactics. Plain and simple.

If the enemy takes the high ground, take it away from him. There was no higher morality involved in that decision. It was simply the right tactical choice to make. Deny the enemy any advantages. If the enemy made a living through a certain commodity, deny the enemy that commodity. It had nothing to do with Sunday-school labeling of right and wrong—it was all tactics. It was whatever would hurt the enemy the most in all the right places. *That* was the name of the game, sure.

After all the miles and the bloodshed, Mack Bolan had to admit that "morality" was a human construct that didn't exist in the world outside of the human cranium. In the real world, morality was nothing more than that which survived. In Nature, that which promoted survival and the perpetuation of more life on earth—that was *right* in the eyes of Nature.

As the helicopter swooped over the wreckage and devastation in the water, Bolan noticed for the first time the huge silver knife-blade shape of the superyacht in the cold gray ocean, plowing through the flotsam like an ice breaker clearing a path.

Harmon saw the yacht, too. "Colonel, I hope those squid are staying deep in the day or that boat is going to be history," she said.

Bolan, aka Colonel Pollock, could see people on the platform running to the big thick glass windows that ringed every level of the environmental sandwich. The people seemed very alarmed at the sight of that yacht approaching. The faces of those people, mostly hard-eyed men, were giddy with dread and excitement. Bolan even glimpsed a group handing money back and forth, probably betting on the odds that the vessel would even make it into the remains of Cassiopeia's harbor before being twisted apart like saltwater taffy and the "goodies" inside removed.

The helicopter lifted and cleared the flight deck of the platform, twisted in the air to face a reception party and landed. As soon as the skids scraped the concrete slab, Bolan had the passenger door open and jumped down, throwing the strap on his photographer's equipment bag over his right shoulder. The greeting party was made up of one guy who looked as if he hadn't checked the weather before getting dressed and a phalanx of Cassiopeia security troops. The troops were dressed in black insulated jumpsuits, no-slip assault boots, black baseball caps and body armor under matching black nylon assault vests. The troops were toting Uzi automatic subguns on lanyards. The buttstocks on the room brooms were fully extended, to give the shooter much more control and accuracy when firing in bursts.

The underdressed guy was wearing a green Hawaiian shirt that was soaked by the hurricane rains whipped up in the rotor wash of the helicopter. His khaki shorts were cuffed and hemmed at the knees. His feet were bare inside a pair of Birkenstock sandals.

The guy jogged through the rotor blast to meet Bolan halfway. Harmon and West were disembarking behind him, shouldering their duffels after jumping down to the wet concrete. They stayed in the background, letting Bolan make the opening plays.

The guy took Bolan's hand and shook it firmly. He seemed completely comfortable soaking wet in this damp chill. If he was cold at all, he was good at hiding the fact.

"Hi! Link Dandridge. I'm Cassiopeia's internal security consultant. I take it you are that high-speed photographer for—?"

"*National Geographic,*" Bolan finished for him.

"But it's Devlin Devereau, right?"

"I just go by Devereau. Make sure everybody understands that, okay?"

Dandridge chuckled as if he were enjoying an inside joke. Bolan's combat instincts were starting to itch. Five more lifts were landing in the foreground near the hangars. Each bird was carrying ten hardguys recruited on the mainland by Leo Turrin. The torpedoes were toting big stainless-steel rifle cases or crates of stolen military munitions.

Bolan narrowed his gaze at what he was seeing downrange. "So, what's your plan, Mr. Security Consultant? Just going to let the kneecapper squad start throwing bombs into the water?"

"That might end up being a contingency. Why don't you let me worry about the tactical sitrep and you can take pictures of it, okay? If the sci-fi team here can't come up with anything more effective, I'll try throwing bombs into the water. Maybe it'll scare them off while killing a bunch of them."

"Well, I just hope that the concrete legs holding this thing out of the water don't crumble into dirt when you start throwing blocks of C-4 around."

Dandridge's eyes widened. He hadn't thought about that particular angle.

Dandridge felt the color red creeping into his peripherals, tasted it in his spit like blood. Goddamned if this guy wasn't skunking him on his own turf. That was the truly infuriating part. The bastard's last remark had extra zing to it; the guy was right.

He turned and smacked the trooper right behind him.

"Go get positive control of that mob, soldier. You tell them that the first man to start dynamiting the harbor will be shot on sight. Got it? No bombs in the water!"

It was Bolan's turn to chuckle.

Dandridge glared, then dismissed the action photographer by stepping away and confronting the two quiet scientists. He looked both of them up and down, his gaze remaining longer on Mallory Harmon.

"And you are?"

"I'm Dr. Abbi Bainbridge," Harmon said. "My associate is Dr. James Solo. We're from Woods Hole Oceanographic Institute."

Mack Bolan was wondering at what point exactly that this whole cover thing would crash.

"We understand that you have an *Architeuthis* problem in these waters. Killed some people, did it?" West asked.

"A what kind of problem?"

Harmon jumped back in. "Don't worry about the Latin. We're experts on this particular species. It's just too damn bad we can't lure a couple of pods of sperm whales into this area. *Architeuthis* is a sperm whale's favorite appetizer. Unfortunately, the sperm whale has been all but harpooned into extinction."

It didn't look like any lights were going on in Link Dandridge's head.

Maybe the April chill to the North Atlantic air was starting to seep through the act. "All right, whatever. You two sound like you know what we're dealing with here."

"Oh, no," Harmon countered. "We're guessing about what it is we're dealing with here. Science only knows that *Architeuthis* exists. Beyond that, we're making big guesses. With the destruction we've seen, I think the passive-aggressive predator debate has been settled. I think we want to find a way on the international front to make sure all the other squid at the bottom of the ocean stay down there."

Dandridge was starting to get a picture now. "These things are big squid?"

"*Giant* squid, Mr. Dandridge. Some of the ones here now are probably over one hundred feet long."

"You think there's a hell of a lot more of them out there? Like if we get rid of this bunch, another group might come up later on?"

"That is a distinct possibility. The Atlantic is the lair of *Architeuthis dux.* I would like to make a prediction. I think we'll start seeing more and more of these monsters prowling near the surface in the future. They're coming up from the bottom because they're experiencing a squid population explosion down there. They've hunted all the food available two miles down and are forced up to find better hunting. Humanity has almost killed off the only predator big and powerful enough to eat *Architeuthis*."

"That would be the sperm whale," Dandridge supplied.

"Exactly. Since the sperm whale hasn't been able to keep the balance, the balance is being thrown into this B-movie nightmare. Humankind better start coughing up the money it's going to take to start cloning sperm whales by the millions."

She motioned at Bolan with a flourishing hand movement.

"Hey, Devereau! Don't you think you should be getting these conversations down on video? We *are* making a documentary here!"

Bolan couldn't believe that the woman had actually hollered at him like that. He could see that this strawberry blonde was a loose cannon when given any kind of operational latitude.

A Motorola two-way radio that Dandridge was carrying in the breast pocket of the rude Hawaiian shirt crackled to life.

"Tiger Bait to Tiger Shark. Hey, Link! That damn yacht made it all the way in! They're puttin' a dinghy in the water now, and it looks like they're going to try to come aboard. What should we do? Should we let them come up?"

Dandridge snatched the radio out of his breast pocket, keying it and thus jamming the entire net until he thought of something to send. The intervention of the radio net broke the stare down between Bolan and Dandridge.

"Ah, how many in the boat, over?"

"I'm looking them over in the binos…five. Two women. Two very fine women."

"What about the guys? They packing? Over?"

"Nothing visually. They might have pistols under their dinner jackets. I wonder if they know that formal wear night has been canceled?"

"All, right, here's what you do. Let them come aboard. Keep them in the lounge till I get there. I'm coming down with the experts." He looked at Bolan and the two scientists, all on the soggy side of sopping wet.

"Who knows, Devereau?" Dandridge said. "You might end up liking this action-photographer gig so much, you might decide to change career paths. What do you think? Weirder shit's happened before."

The Executioner replied, "Link, I think that your whole definition of weird is about to be redefined."

"Yeah? Whatever. Let's get out of this drizzle," Dandridge said.

He spun on sandal-tips and led the way down off the flight deck. Bolan pulled a digital still camera out of his bag, moving the big stainless-steel Desert Eagle .50 AE handgun out of the way to get to it. The armory decided to send him out with the biggest auto in the world for a field test. Bolan's .44 version of the big Israeli autoloader was deadlined for the installation of a new trigger package. The digital camera was top of the line spy equipment. It was a little bigger than the best money could buy commercially but had an image storage capacity of 1.44 gigabytes. Bolan started taking pictures with the eyes of an intelligence officer building an OOB—order of battle—jacket on a target.

West leaned in close to Harmon and whispered,

"An impressive ad-libbing of knowledge on this species, Dr. Harmon. Where did you learn so much about this creature?"

"I read Peter Benchley's last novel. It was about a giant squid."

She giggled and winked. He could tell that she was absolutely beside herself with joy at this dangerous charade they were involved in with people who looked like seasoned killers.

THE LOUNGE WAS serving as the troop command post and the dormitory for the visiting guns. The newcomers didn't get what the excitement was all about. Some of them were at the monster bay windows that were weather-rated up to a Force 12-storm velocity on the Beaufort Scale. There hadn't been a storm in recorded meteorological history bigger than that. On the hurricane intensity scale, the glass slabs were rated to withstand atmospheric and oceanic violence "well in excess of a Category 5 storm." The hurricane scale only went up to 5. But a 5 was a civilization killer. Those concrete supports would probably be blasted to gravel long before the windows ever buckled.

Most of the street soldiers on loan to Cassiopeia were more interested in the sandwich bar in the lounge and, once armed with a double-decker, headed for the scattered stages being manned by Cassiopeian dancers and hookers. Barrel-chested Italians and Sicilians in bright checkerboard-pattern wool shirts and cotton-blend Chino trousers milled around in cliques, talking in hushed tones about the fancy spread the Outfit had out here, about the girls and mostly about how they were being paid well to do nothing.

Level Six was actually bilevel. The upper level was the lounge-main bar area. The decor was industrial modern, with lots of polished brass and stainless steel. Comfortable booths and tables were grouped like villages and islands across the length and width of the deck. A gigantic multilevel bar area included more seating. The place could probably seat three thousand and have lots of elbowroom left for the people who liked to caravan around the room on foot, drinks and drugs in hand.

A specially treated wood deck ringed the lounge for an unobstructed view of the water.

The lower level was almost all dance floor. Two bars spanned the length of the north-south glass faces. There was limited seating along the bars. Several large square sections of the dance floor were actually the same thick glass in the bay windows.

A hired shooter wearing a black crew-neck sweater, blue jeans, a shoulder holster bulging with a large frame revolver, and fishing waders was chowing down on a huge sandwich, looking through the glass between his feet at the dinghy approaching an intact section of dock that was hooked to the starboard stairway. The little rubber boat bounced off pieces of hull drifting like obstacles, the floating destruction left from the predawn attack.

Tiger Bait, a.k.a. Jake Lassiter, was away from the assembled command and control equipment set up in the center of the south wall bar. He, also, was watching the dinghy coming in, and he moved from one glass section to the next when the dinghy went out of sight. He had an idea. He raised the radio and keyed it.

"Hey, we should really have some kind of reception party down there."

Several stations came back with what they thought of that idea. Most of the respondents had been present and awake when the predawn attack took place.

"Screw you, Jake."

"I'm staying up here. Those idiots out there could still go down."

"Why don't you get some of these new guys to go down? They're making the big bucks to do stupid shit like that."

"Good idea," Lassiter keyed back. He quickly released the transmit button then keyed it again.

"Hey, Chumbucket. Get some of these apes down the stairs to meet that dinghy. Tell them they don't even have to stop eating their sandwiches. How copy? Over."

CHUMBUCKET WAS in the lounge at the bay window facing the south, watching the anchored yacht through binoculars as it bobbed on modest swells about 150 yards out. No one was on deck.

He lowered the field glasses to answer Lassiter's call.

"Good copy. Wilco."

He turned away from the windows and looked for the closest clique.

"Hey, you guys over there! I got a mission for you! Let's go!"

The men ignored the waving and hollering Chumbucket. He had to physically get into their faces to get the word across.

"Hey! Guys! Come on! I got a mission and you won't have to put down the sandwiches to do it."

He smiled winningly into the faces of hardmen, almost all of them killers.

Then they all shrugged and a couple of them said, "What the hell? We gotta earn this money somehow."

6

Bolan couldn't believe his eyes. They were on a catwalk in the air that was enclosed in glass. The walkway was about twelve feet wide so the large tour groups could comfortably mill around while looking down upon the world's first meth-manufacturing operation using pharmaceutical-grade production controls and quality assurance checks. These opportunity seekers weren't pumping out bathtub crank with the kind of impurities that ruined trips or, worse yet, canceled lives. This was the best high-octane meth available anywhere in the world.

Placards were mounted on the railing of the catwalk, explaining the processes required to make just one thing: methamphetamine. The placard that Bolan was eyeing indicated that the vats below represented the first step in making the Cassiopeia Crank Recipe. This was the electric conversion of the paint thinner toluene into the Class 1 controlled chemical benzaldehyde.

Bolan took a picture of the placard and shot a few more of the manufacturing room below. They were taking tours through this operation! It was like the Disneyland of illegal drugs.

People in lab coats and wearing respirators were diligently checking pressure readouts, temperature readouts and distilling columns on timed reductions. The room was devoted to manufacturing, packaging and storage. The lab workers all had Cassiopeia security shadows. For the size of the operation, it seemed to Bolan that they were a tad understaffed. The workers down there didn't look like they were getting many breaks. Bolan filed that insight away for possible future use.

Link Dandridge was still going back and forth with his man on the radio while storming down the airtight catwalk, oblivious to the activity below. To him, it was all old hat. The Gee-Whiz factor had worn off a long time ago. The Cassiopeia troops escorted Bolan and the two scientists, making sure everybody stayed together and nobody slipped out of sight.

The march along the glass-enclosed catwalk had the feel of an ambush. Like a walk to the gallows. Bolan's combat sense was crackling like live electricity.

He didn't know if that meant their hosts were preparing a nasty surprise somewhere along the way or he was sensing something worse, something that would threaten them all, good and bad alike, out here on the edge of the Bermuda Triangle.

The Executioner was girding for the worst.

THE CASSIOPEIA MARINA had been constructed on the same principles as pontoon bridges. The aluminum dock planks were built into framed sections that were kept afloat by aluminum cylinders full of air. Each section of dock was fastened to the next by bolts and cables. The dock sections could be hooked together and laid out into any conceivable configuration moored in between the platform's five support columns and branching off into the ocean around Cassiopeia.

In the aftermath of the predawn attack, the harbor had been sliced, diced and dragged under. Most of the marina was either gone or floating free in the waters already choked with wreckage from the crushed hulls of at least two hundred pleasure craft.

The only length of dock that was still serviceable ran directly beneath the platform, north to south straight up the middle. The stairway up to the wooden deck surrounding the lounge was undamaged, and the only way down now to the waterline. Originally, there had been four stairways located in each of the cardinal directions and another long section of dock that bisected what was left floating in the early-morning mist. But that was yesterday.

Of the four newcomers detailed to go down onto what was left of the dock, three of them were making the trip. Their fourth guy had suddenly had to answer a call of Nature.

The three men were all part of the New Jersey Mob, and they were way out of their element. They looked as if they'd emerged from the same Neolithic gene pool— bony brows, thick black body hair and the physiques of gorillas. All wore red or green flannel lumberjack shirts and heavy wool cargo pants, as well as fine leather boat shoes that were guaranteed to maintain positive footing on slippery surfaces. The trio sported shoulder holsters that held large-frame revolvers, and all three cradled Benelli M-1 tactical 12-gauge shotguns. These low-level mafiosi had chosen the Benelli for the same reasons the world's best anti-terrorist teams selected the shotgun: its superb recoil characteristics enabled a skilled shooter to fire five rounds accurately in less than a second.

The dock dipped and swayed as the three big men clomped off the stairs. It wasn't the reaction they were quite expecting. In Jersey, everything was concrete and asphalt. Solidity, a sense of terra firma was imparted with each step in any direction. This, on the other hand, was completely unnerving. The floating walkway had obviously had the starch knocked right out of it, and the only thing keeping it from drifting off into the gloom was the stairway they'd just descended.

"Jesus!" Manny Baglio exclaimed as he scrabbled for a handhold on the cable railing located on either side of the walkway. "Can't they stiffen this thing up a little? This is goddamn dangerous!"

"I don't think the problem is the dock. It's what did this *to* the dock," Lou Ventura said.

Vince Ribaldi was looking around at the destruction that disappeared into the misting rain in every direction. "I think Bobby Boy had the right idea. I shoulda gone to take a shit, too."

The small outboard of the approaching dinghy was loud enough now to overpower the soft lapping of the water against the pontoons and the floating debris.

The hunter orange of the boat was easy to lock on to visually under the conditions. The people in the boat were still shadow shapes in the fog, which seemed to be getting thicker.

Lou Ventura was in charge of these men, so he did the communicating between the parties.

"Hey!" he yelled at the color-shapes cutting serpentine tracks through the swells to avoid obstacles. "Ain't you heard? We're closed to all comers! Look at the shit around you, okay? We got a real problem here and we don't want you morons adding to it!"

A strong male voice boomed across the waters. "We are here to offer a way out."

Ventura looked at Baglio. "A way out? What fuckin' planet are they from?"

Baglio shrugged. He just wanted to get the hell away from this madness.

"You gonna send them back?" Ribaldi asked.

Ventura thought about it. "Naw. I figure they've earned the right, making it this far."

Ribaldi turned white. His eyes widened and he started licking his lips compulsively. "What do you mean? You mean whatever did this could still be around?"

Ventura looked at him as if he were from Mars. "Hey, genius. We're out here 'cause whatever did this is probably still out here. Get it? Remember *Jaws?* Well, we been hired to go get the shark. Get the picture?"

Ribaldi didn't like the picture, but he kept quiet about it. His eyes were wandering, watching the water for clues of anything terrible.

The dinghy was close enough now to see the faces that belonged to the shapes. The two women were dressed formally and in stark contrast. The blond looker wore a white cocktail dress with white hose and heels. The slit up the side of the dress went almost to her hip. Her brunette companion was dressed in scarlet red with the same colored accessories. The man in the bow was tall and lean, and he was dressed in black. It wasn't until the dinghy was bumping into the dock and a rope line was thrown into Ventura's chest that he saw the man was wearing a Catholic priest's garb—but this man's collar was black.

To all three shooters standing on the rickety dock, all of them born and raised Catholic, the image of that black collar was like looking at evil for the first time. It just wasn't right. And the fact that this dude was parading around in public like that spoke volumes about who he was serving. And it probably wasn't the Man upstairs. Ribaldi was really eyeballing the water now.

Ventura almost dropped his Benelli as he slapped with his free hand to grab the line that had been pitched into his chest. Reflexively, he tied off the line to the top cable of the railing.

The man in black said, "Coming aboard."

He stepped up from the bow of the dinghy, mounted the lower rung on the cable railing and threw his legs over. Baglio and Ribaldi scrambled to hoist the women over the cable rails and onto the spongy footing of the dock. The coxswain stayed with the outboard engine. A man wearing a gray trench coat, brown suit and horn-rimmed glasses and clutching a leather briefcase scaled the railing without assistance and landed on the dock. The slight man with thinning hair seemed unaccustomed to this kind of travel. He was being dragged along out of necessity. To the mafiosi, he was instantly tagged as a useful outsider. He wasn't made like the girls and the evil priest were.

The man in black was looking up appreciatively at the massive underside of the Cassiopeia platform.

"Is the man of the house in?" he asked.

Ventura thought that was just damned funny. "The man of the house? He just floats up and wants the man of the house. Who do you think you are? Some kinda royalty?"

The man with the hard-lined face smiled. "I am descended from the black royalty of Europe, but I have renounced all titles and privileges of that bloodline. Is there going to be a problem with having the audience we've come to seek?"

Ventura pulled the two-way radio out of his pocket and keyed the transmit button.

"Hey, Tiger Shark, somebody in charge up there get on the horn. This is Lou. We're down on the dock with the visitors. I need some instructions."

A burst of static was followed by a nasal voice.

"This is Tiger Shark. Go ahead, Lou. What have you got?"

Ventura wondered how he should describe this bunch. Or if he even should. "I've got a man here descended from royalty no less that wants to see the man of the house. What do you want me to do with them?"

"You've got five people down there, right?"

"Four that want to come up. One guy is still in the boat. Looks like he's gonna stay where he's at."

"Send them up with one of your guys. Two of you stay down there and keep an eye on the boatman. Got it?"

"Yeah, I got it."

Ribaldi was immediately volunteering to go up with the visitors. "I'll take them up, Lou. Okay?"

Ventura could see the fear in Vince's eyes. It didn't move him with sympathy.

"Manny," he said, "take the royal family up top. Vince and I will keep their boy here on ice until they come back."

Ribaldi practically screeched, "But, Lou—!"

"Hey, you're actin' like a goddamn chicken, Vince. It's makin' me sick."

Ribaldi decided to suck it up and drive on. It wasn't good for a reputation if Lou got it into his head that somebody was yellow, that they didn't have a good set of legs to stand on.

"Get them up top, Manny," Ventura said.

7

San Diego, California

As the sun was creeping across the Appalachians bringing light to the sky, it would still be almost two hours before sunrise in California. The parking lot of the Windjammers Motel was quiet. The sounds of the nearby ocean, the unseen crickets and the hum of electricity bleeding off the halogen lamps illuminating the lot created a strangely soothing symphony.

The car was sitting in front of door number 3—a late 70s model Chevy Impala that was wanted for emissions violations, unpaid parking fines and brake lights that didn't work. The car stereo worked. It was stolen merchandise that had changed hands five times before ending up in the primer red Impala parked in the Windjammers lot at quarter to four in the morning.

The driver was acting as a combination lookout and front door guard. He was listening to Ice T raps on a much lower volume setting than he would have liked. Tendrils of smoke from a cherry-flavored cigarillo that had been emptied of tobacco and repacked with marijuana curled up to the roof of the sedan. The street term for the reeking stick was a blunt.

The man behind door number 3 was known on the streets as Rock Dog, and he was the leader of the Blood set called the Eighty-Deuce, which ran all oceanside action in San Diego. Rock Dog was a known sympathizer and supporter of the Islam Nation. While the strict brand of Islam practiced by the Nation forbade drug peddling, vice, dirty living and killing your brothers, Rock Dog was a large cash contributor to the weekly collection. The financial support garnered him a lot of leeway in the lifestyle department. Rock Dog's set was employed on many occasions in after hours attacks on the white devils that enslaved the black man to crack and welfare.

The fact that Rock Dog's set was the major crack distributor in San Diego didn't seem to raise any eyebrows over this conflict of interest. Rock Dog didn't like whitey and that was what counted. What the brothers in the Nation didn't know about was Rock Dog's addiction to the white devil's women.

Thus the sneaking around at 3:00 a.m. with guards posted outside the rendezvous. He couldn't let word of his white girl habit get out.

The lookout in the Impala didn't see the dark-clothed figure slip up alongside the car until a shadow crossed his face. He peered out the rolled-down window with a start. He recognized a man-shape before his eyes bugged and his jaws clenched violently. His fingers lost feeling, and he couldn't let go of the steering wheel. His assailant had a black box mashed into his beefy neck, and the crackle of electricity was like swarming wasps inside his head. After a good ten-second burst at 300,000 volts, Mr. Blunt was in no condition to fight back, let alone move. The driver's door was opened, and the dark figure pulled the gangbanger out of the car and flopped him facedown on the pavement. Blunt's arms were jerked behind his back and some kind of plastic banding was cinched around his crisscrossed wrists, effectively restraining him. Then the gangster was dragged behind the car and left facedown under the bumper.

The cops would have no problem finding him like that.

The wraith knelt and whispered into Blunt's ear. "Can you hear me?"

A nod from pavement level that was almost imperceptible in the deep shadows.

"What's the code to bail out?"

Blunt was blinking with confusion. His brains were still popping off sparklers in the wake of being fried with the stun gun.

"Whhaa?"

"I said, what is the code to tell your buddy to bail out?"

"Fhuck shew, maan."

The little black box was put in front of his face. With a press of a button, a little bolt of lightning came to life and danced between two electrodes.

"You want to do the dying cockroach again?"

The lightning bolt licked wickedly before his eyes.

"It's up to you. My next jolt is going in your ball sac. I'll juice you until your testicles explode. Do you understand that?"

Gravel scraped as the gangster nodded again.

"What's the code, Blood? Don't piss me off now."

"Honk da horn once."

"That's it?"

"Dat's it."

"Thank you. Cooperating can be so much less painful."

The shadow figure stood, went back to the open car door, reached inside and leaned on the horn once. Then the figure moved swiftly onto the sidewalk and flattened against the wall next to door number 3.

The door flew open with a crash and a naked black man with a ball of clothing pressed into his crotch pole-vaulted out of the room and jumped up on the hood of the car to make a leap for the passenger side. Strong fingers jerked the gang leader backward by the cornrows, spinning him. A shoe in his back slammed him face first into the brick wall of the motel. His nose exploded and stars flared in his brain. The strong hand at his neck pulled him back and cracked his skull into the brick again.

His legs became rubber and his body sagged. The dark-clad figure hugged the gangster from behind and dragged him into the parking lot. A red Taurus sedan pulled away from the curb, lights out, and rolled quietly into the parking lot. The trunk automatically popped open, and the dark figure deposited the unconscious crack dealer on top of the spare tire and secured his arms behind his back with a plastic band. The figure slammed the trunk and got into the sedan on the passenger side.

In the car, Johnny Bolan sighed.

The driver, an off-duty Beverly Weaver, asked, "Where to?"

"I've got a safehouse rented up in the hills. Let's get on the freeway and I'll tell you where to go."

"You got it."

She hooked a U-turn and powered out of the parking lot without signaling.

Johnny frowned and said, "Maybe you should call for a car to pick up the one we left behind. I wouldn't want anybody running over him thinking he's a speed bump."

Weaver chuckled. "No, that just wouldn't be proper."

ROCK DOG, a.k.a. Moretha Haakem Benson, boomed
back into consciousness on the vapors of something so
foul that his almost senseless brain couldn't ignore it. He
made a sound like a belch squeezing through a scream
and blinked repeatedly, trying to focus on something. A
murky figure was walking away from him on his left. A
single 60-watt bulb burned overhead with no reflector.
The wattage was too low to banish the shadows. He noticed movement to his front. It was a man with dark hair
moving toward a refrigerator that was pushed against the
unfinished wall of what had to be a basement. Rock
Dog was in an uncomfortable wooden chair, and he was
tied to it from at least seven points of contact.

The man was tall and seemed lithe, although from
behind the flowing long black coat made that determination an impression until he turned. The coat moved
like a cape around the man's moving body; Rock Dog
thought of Dracula and gulped.

The refrigerator door opened and bottles clanked
loudly. The light inside the fridge was burned out. The
man in black was leaning down to consult the inventory
in there, whatever it was. The man asked without turning, "What kind of beer do you prefer, Dog? Domestic
cheap, domestic pricey, microbrew or import?"

Rock Dog registered the word beer. Was this guy
asking him what kind of beer he liked? What kind of
crazy shit was this? Then Rock Dog remembered the alcohol content in beer and blabbered, "Hey, man! I can't
have no beer! The courts put me on somethin' that
makes me sick on the alcohol! I can't drink no beer!"

The man looked back at Rock Dog and smiled.
"Yeah, I'm aware of that. But if you were drinking beer,
what's your poison? Domestic, microbrew or import?"

"Hey, I ain't drinkin' no beer! I tried once! I felt like I was dyin'!"

The man stood and turned completely to face him. Yeah, this guy was lean like a lot of the brothers. The dude was wearing a black turtleneck and black slacks. He had on some kind of black hiking sneaker looking shoes.

"Well, okay, Dog. I'll go along with that. Just tell me who hired you."

"Who hired me? What you mean, white boy?"

"You know what I mean."

"Who hired me for what?"

"You sent a goon squad to grab a stripper named Jazz Mercedes who works at the Matrix."

"I did?"

The man frowned and shook his head. He looked toward Dog's left.

"Bev. The beer bong, please."

Dog realized that a woman was standing in the shadows to his left. That's what he'd seen immediately after opening his eyes—the woman walking away after breaking the smelling salts under his nose. The woman was wearing a navy blue motorcycle cop's jacket with no badge, navy fatigue pants and SWAT team assault boots.

The woman grabbed a large green plastic funnel that was hanging to an exposed stud by a nail. A long clear vinyl tube was affixed to the skinny end of the funnel. It was a frat boy's favorite. The beer bong.

Johnny Bolan pointed at the punk. "Make him suck tube and hold the funnel up high."

Then he began selecting beers. He grabbed one beer from each of the domestic categories and then two microbrews and two imports. An even six. The funnel was big enough to hold eight beers.

Weaver did as instructed. Rock Dog didn't have much choice. He tried to keep his jaws clenched, but with the woman's timely use of the Church Key nerve attack, Dog's jaws were spread wide and screaming in no time. She easily got the tube in between his teeth. She clamped her hands around the hose and Dog's mouth and nose, keeping him from spitting the hose out. Then she held the funnel high.

Johnny was lining up the six-charge on the concrete floor in front of Dog. He took the long neck Stilch's Pilsner, the cheapest of American beers, twisted off the cap and tossed it over Dog's shoulder. It zinged and ricocheted into a corner. He stalked up on Dog with the open beer, smiling, and upended the bottle over the open funnel. The bottle emptied quickly with lots of foam and made burned cold skid marks down the back of Dog's gulping gullet. The gangbanger had no choice but to swallow every drip of that beer. Then unexpectedly, with a martial artist's cry, Johnny smashed the beer bottle between Dog's feet. Rock Dog almost moved his bowels. His eyes rolled up in his head and the beer sloshed around in his guts.

The drugs in his system were waiting for that.

It took a little reaction time. Dog's cappuccino complexion actually seemed to be getting a little green before the eruption. And then—it was like a column of foaming beer and stomach acid under high pressure. His mouth was open and pointing up. Weaver let go of his face as the puke cleared the launch pad and she danced backward out of range. Dog's head drooped to his chest while the fire hose retch purged every molecule of alcohol from the stomach. His abdomen rippled as the muscles clenched violently.

Rock Dog's head hung from his shoulders, chin on chest and he continued to make little pukes into his lap and cough and cry in between gut-twisting efforts. Johnny grabbed a fistful of the cornrows and lifted the gang leader's head.

"Ready for beer number two, Dog?"

"Please! No more!"

"Who hired you to grab the girl, Dog?"

Johnny had to administer three beers before Rock Dog crackled like flaky shale. Anabuse was nothing to try to defy. Its reaction with beer made an excellent incentive to start talking.

HAVING COME from the top down, Bolan had quite a master file ready to be sent by encrypted burst transmission over the satcom back to Stony Man Farm. The Executioner had left standing instructions that Able Team was to be tasked with follow-on to this mission as soon as the team touched down in Virginia. Finding a secure perch to put in that call was going to be Bolan's next priority.

While shooting the intel photos, his mind had been working on the problem of Link Dandridge and what the guy represented. Bolan was reading Dandridge as a Company asset. Which meant that Dandridge was an actual employee of the CIA, not just a contract agent. The man from CIA was making no effort to hide the fact that he thought Bolan was a phony. So there had to be a leak somewhere. At some point, there was going to be a confrontation about those suspicions. Somebody would stop living as a result. Bolan was going to do what he had to do to make sure that somebody wasn't him.

Many good men in government had looked at the CIA and come to the conclusion that the Company was completely out of control. What did a man of conscience and patriotism do when the perception finally filtered through that his own government had a dark and evil underbelly? This was increasingly becoming Mack Bolan's dilemma. His survival record on the battlefield was largely the result of his ability to be utterly realistic about his enemies. Treating all white hats as untouchable because of their job or government affiliation was unrealistic. Bolan had let some bad apples walk away with their lives in the past simply because those men were carrying a badge. In retrospect, he should have executed them as surely as any Mafia chieftain he'd ever dropped the hammer on. The blood of innocents on any cop's hands wasn't somehow absolved by the badge.

Nobody was above Bolan's brand of jungle law.

On the refined scale of predators, Link Dandridge didn't feel like one of the True Believer crowd. This man Cassandra fit that bill much more than Dandridge ever would. Dandridge was an opportunist, not a visionary. He was the kind of rat that was totally wrapped up in keeping the greedy little game of me in perpetual motion. He liked his fun and games. He wanted to make sure that, above all else, the fun and games continued without any interference from outsiders.

But a rat was a rat. No matter how you dressed him up for dinner.

And the devil was always in the details.

Bolan recognized immediately that the man wearing the suit of a priest but with a black collar was making more than a fashion statement. That outfit was more like a badge of office. A bold statement of purpose and place in the greater universe. A station in life that probably had very little to do with altruistic sensibilities. Another cannibal present to stake a claim at the banquet.

Link Dandridge was nobody's idea of a diplomat. He stalked up on the tall, lean man in black and actually snickered. He asked, "Jeez, dude! Does the Pope know you're walking around like that?"

The man considered Dandridge with cool detachment. Bolan had seen that look before. It was the look of wanton superiority gazing upon the house of rabble. It was the look of the cobra to its prey. It was the look of a god considering a meager spark of life with no more importance than an ant underfoot.

Rather than address the remark at all, he merely introduced himself with the soft-spoken manner of a man very used to having his way.

"My name is Wesson Fairchild. I am the custodian of the Bermuda Conservatory. I represent a consortium of interests very concerned with what is going on out here."

"Yeah? What exactly is going on out here to interest your consortium?"

"Are you the man of the house here?"

"What?"

Bolan spoke up. "He's asking if you're the top dog around here."

"Is that what he's asking? And who asked you?"

Wesson Fairchild could see that Dandridge wasn't the man he needed to confront.

"I will not speak my concerns to an underling. I will have an audience with the man of the house. I'm not leaving until that takes place."

Dandridge didn't like being reduced to the status of

mere underling. He just wasn't anybody's bag boy. He was a mover and a shaker, too.

"Better watch your smug mouth, guy. The getup doesn't impress me. I don't care if you've got Satan on your side, to get anything around here you gotta go through me first."

"I understand that little men always see themselves as more than they really are."

"Is that how you understand it? I understand that everyone within eyeshot is carrying a firearm. Everyone that is but you and your two little high society bitches and the mousy looking asshole with the briefcase. I don't have to let you do shit. In fact, I just might throw you and your crew over the railing and make you swim back to your fancy yacht. What do you think of that?"

"I understand that the intended purpose of this structure isn't living up to its full potential right now. I understand that the longer this situation drags on, the more money you and yours stand to lose. Every day that you turn people away is another million or two lost forever."

Dandridge worked his jaws on that point. He didn't have a snappy comeback, but if this guy was offering his expertise, that was already covered.

"Well, we've already got experts for that. See these three?" Dandridge indicated Bolan, Harmon and West. "Well, two of them are experts anyway."

Fairchild turned his gaze on Bolan and his contract operatives. He was like the man with X-ray eyes. He looked, he saw, then he smiled. And returned his flinty eyes back on Dandridge.

"To people like you, people like them are very problematic," he said.

Dandridge's eyes narrowed. Bolan was stowing the

camera gear and fisting the Desert Eagle inside the photo bag. It was one of those moments.

Dandridge looked at Bolan and back at Fairchild.

"What do you mean exactly?"

"I mean that these three will always do what is right. You will always do what is in your best interest. It's all a matter of perspective."

"That's neat," Dandridge said. "I like perspective. It's definitely time to get some perspective around here."

The five Cassiopeia troops that had been chaperoning the three "VIPs" since stepping off the helicopter had Bolan in a human cul-de-sac. All of them had quietly taken up this horseshoe configuration around the Executioner without telegraphing anything sinister or out of place. They seemed bored and uninterested in anything going on. Until he saw Dandridge look over his shoulder at the troops and give them an almost imperceptible nod.

Five metallic clicks sounded as the safeties went off and the muzzles came up, all weapons trained on Bolan's skull.

Dandridge laughed. "That's a better perspective already. Hey, Devereau. Like, take your hand out of the bag. Very slowly, okay? That's a good boy. Now hand me the bag."

Bolan was mentally kicking himself over this reversal. Someone in the CIA had more intel on Bolan than Stony Man was aware of. That leak would have to be plugged somehow. He'd leave that up to Hal.

The most disturbing part of this situation was the fact that Leo had come to Bolan with the mission. These bastards knew enough to make the approach through somebody that Bolan trusted absolutely. That kind of savvy intelligence had to come from somewhere.

Bolan did as he was told. It was suicide to do otherwise. He knew that Dandridge wouldn't kill him immediately. Guys like him had to gloat first. There was a ritual that had to be observed. There'd be questions and torture. Bolan had to figure he'd worked up quite a tab over the years interfering with and actively opposing Company operations around the world.

It was time to pay the piper.

8

Forty-seven Miles Due East of
Cassiopeia Territorial Waters

The submarine was on the surface and holding position at the designated coordinates. The misting rain reduced visibility to less than a mile, and a light breeze was whispering from the west.

Captain Dominick "Nick" Chance stayed with the conn in the control center while his first officer, Commander Len Shaw, supervised the boarding of the covert team from the bridge. This special three-man unit wasn't from the Army, Navy or Marines. They weren't with the Company. But they came with the highest authorization from the National Command Authority. Which was a fancy way of saying that the President himself was green-lighting this operation from the White House.

Nick Chance was the youngest captain in the submarine fleet. At thirty-three, command of the most sophisticated attack submarine in the U.S. Navy was an earned achievement. There had been nothing political at all in his appointment. He was a brilliant tactician and a man whose daring didn't seem to have many limits. The stunt that earned him the rank of captain and gave him his newest command was legend now among the men of the "silent service." It was during a joint NATO-Russian Federation exercise and Chance was commanding an improved Los Angeles-class boat. Chance's mission was the same as every other participant's in the exercise: find the Typhoon-class boomer that was in the hands of separatists and sink her before she could launch her missiles against targets in the U.S.

Chance had put himself in the deck shoes of the boomer's skipper and reasoned where that sub would be to avoid the NATO-Russian forces looking for her. Rather than making a flank charge across the Atlantic for its targets, the boomer went north under the ice cap and crossed over to the Canadian side, then turned south and shadowed the coastline, completely avoiding the naval task forces looking for her. Chance was waiting for the boomer just below the Arctic Circle between Newfoundland and Greenland. Prior to his current command, the improved Los Angeles-class boat was the quietest submarine in the world.

Rather than announcing his presence to the rogue boomer with a shooting solution that would have ended the exercise, Chance shadowed the missile sub along the Canadian coast and waited for her to jettison weighted cans of trash to the bottom—a noisy operation on any submarine. At that point, he floated a radio buoy that notified the hunters of the boomer's location. The Russian ships arrived first and scored the kill. Chance's boat remained undetected by the boomer and her hunters. With the kill scored, the exercise was terminated and the boomer was ordered back to her home port at Petropavlovsk. Chance followed the boomer back across the Atlantic, and nobody knew that he was there until he surfaced his boat practically alongside the monster Russian submarine inside the submarine base.

It was a cowboy stunt that earned him both a reprimand and the Navy's highest decoration for bravery and valor. They gave him his eagles and the most advanced nuclear attack submarine ever put to sea: USS *Seawolf*. *Seawolf* was the first boat in a class of three bearing the same name. She was the quietest, fastest and biggest nuclear attack submarine in the world.

It was quite an accomplishment for a farm boy from Iowa.

Nick Chance was six feet tall and a lean two hundred pounds of loyalty-inspiring leader. There was a waiting list of officers and enlisted men who wanted the opportunity to serve with him. Only the best of the best served with Chance, and he handpicked his crew.

He was standing on the raised periscope platform at the OOD—officer of the deck—watch station located in the center of the control room. To his rear were two periscopes mounted side by side. To his front he had full view of the *Seawolf*'s status boards. To his left was ship's control and on his right was fire control. He was waiting on a report from the bridge.

Overhead, the speaker box squawked. "Conn, bridge. This is the XO. One MH-53 Pave Low helicopter on low level approach bearing niner-three."

Chance reached up and plucked the mike from its fixture. "Bridge, conn. Acknowledged. Clear the bridge as soon as the VIPs are onboard."

"Conn, bridge. Affirmative."

Chance couldn't hear the helicopter through the pressure hull. He relied upon his XO to be his eyes and ears. After another minute, the report came back.

"Conn, bridge. VIPs are onboard. Forward escape trunk is secure."

"Clear the bridge."

"Aye, sir. Clearing the bridge."

"Sonar, conn. Sounding."

Sonar reported back. "Conn, sonar. Sounding. One-three-one fathoms."

Through the forward hatch, Chance heard the XO and his two lookouts clanging down the ladder from the bridge above. He heard the XO yell, "XO down!"

Len Shaw was three inches taller than the captain. He had to stoop to get through the hatches in any submarine. The African-American commander had declined an offer to play pro ball to join the Navy as a submarine officer. It was a decision he'd never regretted.

As Commander Shaw entered the control room from the forward hatch, Chance nodded at him and smiled.

"XO, submerge the ship."

Shaw nodded and turned toward the ship's control station. The senior enlisted man, Tad Dillinger, was the chief of the boat and manned the diving officer's position directly behind the bucket seats occupied by the planesman and helmsman. The chief of the boat was always addressed as "Cob."

"Cob, submerge the ship. Make your depth two-five-zero feet."

Dillinger echoed the command. "Make my depth two-five-zero feet, aye, sir. Chief of the watch on the one MC—dive! Dive!"

Those words echoed via speakers throughout the submarine.

To the two enlisted sailors manning the helm and planes controls he said, "Make your depth two-five-zero feet. Five degree down bubble."

The chief of the watch manned the controls for trim and ballast. The vents were opened to allow a measured amount of water into the ballast tanks to make the submarine slightly heavier than water and sink beneath the waves. This condition was called "negatively buoyant." The air escaping from the ballast tanks made an audible hissing through the hull and the deck sloped at a moderate angle as the submarine gracefully plunged beneath the surface of the gray Atlantic.

Chance said, "Mr. Shaw, please see to our guests and escort them to the control room."

"Aye, sir."

The Cassiopeia Platform

MACK BOLAN HAD BEEN separated from his comrades and shoved at muzzle-point into the full service kitchen area. The skeleton crew running the kitchen was put on a break until further notice and sent above to play in the casino or hash dens. The white smocked chefs didn't need to be told twice. From the looks in their eyes, Bolan surmised that similar dismissals had taken place in the past.

Link Dandridge threw Bolan's photo bag on a stainless-steel cutting table and said, "Take a seat, pal."

"I'd rather stand."

Dandridge looked at one of his storm troopers. "Pull up a seat for this ass wipe and make him sit."

The trooper nodded and pulled a metal chair out of the break area. Two soldiers used their boot heels and cracked Bolan in the back of the knees. His legs buckled and he dropped into the seat.

Dandridge returned his attention to the photo bag and unzipped it.

"Let's see what we have in here."

Dandridge whistled and his eyes widened. He hefted the massive silver handgun out of the bag and looked it over. He popped the magazine, eyed the loads and slammed it back into the grip again.

"What's a photographer need with artillery like this?"

"I deal with dangerous animals. Sometimes I have to shoot more than pictures in order to keep from being lunch."

Dandridge chuckled. "I bet."

Dandridge set the .50 Desert Eagle on the table and went back to rifling through Bolan's stuff. He plunked the digital camera next to the handgun, then a laptop and then he pulled out and stacked up fifteen extra magazines for the hand cannon.

"No film, Dev. Why's that?"

"Digital camera. Don't need any."

"Ah. Why all the reloads? Don't you respect animals?"

"Maybe you need to take a look around your harbor again. Frankly, I don't think that's going to be big enough. I just couldn't get a bazooka in the bag."

Dandridge chuckled again. He began to feel the sides of the bag. A zippered compartment on the side contained something large. He unzipped the compartment and looked inside.

"I'm sure there's a logical explanation for this piece of equipment, Dev."

There was no conceivable reason for a wildlife photographer to be packing a highly classified LST-5C satcom transceiver. The radio was a small black box that weighed about ten pounds. Covert operators were the only people fielding this device. The jig was up.

Bolan frowned. "Photography is my day job."

Dandridge laughed heartily. "Busted."

"Okay, Dandridge. Enough of the bullshit. Who tipped you off?"

"Nobody. I brought you here. Your cover was compromised from the minute your Fed friend contacted you."

"You're Company, aren't you?"

"I'll ask the questions. Who's the crew you're working with?"

"They're marine biologists. Completely legit."

"Sure they are. You might as well tell me. I'll torture it out of them, too."

"Is there anybody in the Company worth a shit anymore?"

"Your problem is you're fighting for an America that doesn't exist anymore."

"Yeah, I've noticed this shift toward becoming the land of fascists and thugs. It's no wonder the rest of the world hates our guts. With clowns like you representing our interests overseas it's easier to understand what all the resentment is about."

"We are the future."

"Your future's not going to make it."

"*You're* the one who's not going to make it. It's not going to be quick. You're going to tell us everything. I've got a couple of the Outfit's best interrogators on the payroll, and I'm turning them loose on you."

Despite himself, Bolan felt the cold wash of anxiety

sluice through his guts at the mention of the Mob interrogators. He'd seen too much of their brand of handiwork over the years. If this mission was going to be the final one, Mack Bolan wasn't going to draw his last breath screaming insanely from inside a body turned turkey. He'd force them to blow his brains out before it came to that. He had all those weapons trained on his head right now. All he had to do was make a sudden, threatening move and he knew the troops would do the rest.

Bolan's grim speculations were literally short-circuited from behind. One of the five troops behind him rammed a stun gun into Bolan's back between the shoulder blades. The stunning voltage that was blasting through his nervous system seized up every muscle in his body. He wasn't capable of gasping or crying out. Pop rockets of bleached gold that drizzled into blood compromised his vision. That threatening move was out of the question now. He was welded into the chair.

He was aware of something thumping into the side of his body suddenly and violently. A boot to the ribs. The floor went vertical and a whitewashed world capsized. He was tumbling but there was merciful relief. His nervous system was firing on its own again. The light was fading and there was another impact—bigger and heavier this time.

He sensed more than saw the men falling on him, dropping with weight behind a knee into sensitive, potentially fatal target areas of the body and each hand buried the electrodes on identical black pistol grips into his kidneys, neck, back and crotch.

His mind was still managing to hang on to consciousness by a couple of fingernails. He had no impression of the jolt of electricity this time being five times worse than the first. It was an electric white light orchestra inside his head and then his head, his body, his entire reception of the universe was gone.

Dandridge breathed a sigh of relief. He was coiled with adrenaline on this guy's reputation alone. It seemed incredible that this walking myth could fall so easily. With no casualties to boot.

He frowned and cocked his head toward the meat locker.

"Tape his wrists and hang him from a hook. Send a guy out to get Matt and Mark. Tell them to bring their turkey kits. I got a holiday bird just waiting for their special touch."

MALLORY HARMON'S eyes tracked the two grim individuals packing large suitcases. A lone black-clad security soldier was escorting the gorilla twins into the kitchen. She wasn't sure what made her more nervous, the knowledge of what was going to be taking place in the kitchen or the specter of what the brown-eyed psychopath might do to her if he decided that she was worth the risk.

She knew that cowboy tactics at this point were out of the question. The situation was beyond grave. Everything now had to be played exactly on key or they'd end up in the kitchen, too.

When the tables had turned and the colonel had been taken at muzzle point through the swing doors back there, Dandridge had lingered enough to assign Brown Eyes this detail. He had two of his boys in backup. Each of them was cradling a pump shotgun. The action at their table was starting to attract a crowd.

Harmon was the woman most likely to end up as fair game for this mob. The dancers on stage were protected property. Brown Eyes was meticulously searching through her duffel. When he found her undergarments, his arousal was obvious. And when she saw that, everything about the man was an open book.

This aberration of male behavior was on a loop. The arousal at the sight of her undergarments was the first step in a neurological escalator that would end in murder and rape. She had to scramble that pattern fast. There was only one way to do that.

Engage in something outrageous.

She looked over at Donovan West like a mentor to a gifted protégé. "It always starts with our panties."

She made the statement sound as if West knew exactly what she was saying. West had seen enough of her behavior to know that she was winging it again. He gave her the stage by saying nothing.

Her statement had an effect on Brown Eyes. He was mentally reviewing a checklist that had blown up in his face. The woman wasn't responding as she should.

She should be scared into begging for the terms of her own violation.

"What?"

Her eyes were like needles poking into his soul. "You started out worshiping us, didn't you?"

The question ricocheted through his brain and didn't find a receptor. His eyes blinked out vacancy while his mind spun like the wheels in a slot machine.

"What?"

She explained it to West. She still hadn't even acknowledged the sex killer's presence as a human being.

As Brown Eyes listened to her words, he hadn't ever felt so unbalanced, so much out of control.

She acknowledged him now and brought him right into the center of this vortex.

"What was your mother like?" she asked. Her tone was designed to convey confidentiality and understanding.

"She was cold. She made me feel bad."

"You've had an above average interest in the differences between us."

"Yes."

"She made you feel like it was wrong. Your mother made you feel like a woman's body unclothed was a sin. Am I right?"

"Yes."

"You've only wanted to get to know us, is that right?"

The blinking of his eyes was frantic. West was beyond speechless watching this exchange. What in the hell kind of voodoo magic was this?

"It might make you feel better if we talked about this in a place with a little more privacy. Would that make you feel more at ease?"

Harmon could tell by what his eyes were doing that the guy was replaying imagery in his mind's eye. Rewinding through the past, looking for something. She had evoked something in him. Something buried and consciously discarded. The part of him that was paying attention to her every word and gesture nodded the head and answered.

"I would like to be alone with you."

Her hand floated up and she squeezed his left elbow.

"When I touch you like this or when you touch yourself like this, you can always find this moment and this feeling of being safe and secure. Doesn't that feel wonderful?"

"Yes."

"Do you want to go there now?"

"Yes."

Her hand was still there and she squeezed again, reinforcing the anchor.

"Are you there now?"

"Yes."

"Show me where it is in this place that makes you feel very safe."

He spun on his toe and started walking toward the main staircase. Harmon followed him. West and the two backups watched them depart. It was a very strange sight. The underworld enforcer walking like a man with a purpose and a clenched fist full of women's undergarments being followed loyally by the woman in question.

West clapped his hands together jovially to break the ice but broke the two men's trances instead. The two torpedoes eyed the tall, lanky scientist with dizzy looks.

"Yes, well, there it is. Gentlemen, you can search my bags. I certainly have nothing to hide, and your supervisor seems satisfied with my colleague."

West opened the athletic bag and chopped it with both hands at each end, fluffing out the innards like a giant baked potato. He slid his bag to the "customs" side of the table. The two of them looked at the bag then back at West, who was busy looking anywhere but at the two torpedoes.

The last thing he wanted to do right now was look like a competing alpha male in the eyes of these two throwbacks. Keep the tail tucked. That was the idea.

9

Damien Cassandra was running out of patience. The east coast was screaming for product. The Five Families were heavily invested in the Cassiopeia project, and the biker sources for crystal had been given the shaft in lieu of a source in which the Mob had a controlling interest. Cassiopeia had the best product in the world due to a revolutionary conversion process involving electricity and the precious metal palladium, but that meant nothing when the product couldn't connect between point A and point B. The alternative was to begin massive airlifts of product off the platform to waiting vessels outside the danger zone.

Switching to airlifts wouldn't be a problem, but it would raise costs. Raising costs was the one factor that couldn't be absorbed in this strategy play for market dominance. The idea was to offer the highest quality full octane meth at a price that undercut the bathtub chemists by twenty percent. Cassandra wanted a situation where the biker brigades were offering product that was higher in price and much lower in grade. They would step into that vacuum with crystal that kicked ass for forty-eight hours straight and sold for twenty dollars less than the best that the red phosphorus chemists could cook at any price. It was a ploy that would force the bikers out of manufacturing and into distribution only.

And Cassiopeia would be the capital. The Amsterdam of meth. Open to all comers. Cassiopeia was the fruition of a lifetime philosophy relentlessly pursued in every action, every breath he'd ever taken. Compromise and strategic alliances made far from the public eye had been the order of the day. It couldn't have been accomplished in any other manner.

Cassandra in no way felt like a traitor to his own ideals for getting into the bed with covert operations and organized crime in order to put Cassiopeia on the map. Now that he'd been at the helm of his own ship of state for almost six months, he could see that he needed to find a more "republican" minded liaison from the Company than Dandridge. Dandridge was making it clear that he saw the Cassiopeia Republic as nothing more than another clever front owned and operated by the Central Intelligence Agency. Dandridge had been installed into the Cassiopeian government as the Secretary of National Security.

When Cassandra was drafting the Cassiopeian Constitution, the CIA insisted that the post be given autonomous control of the military, and that a Company man filled the post. Cassandra swallowed his anger and vented it privately. He had no choice but to accept the dictate from the CIA and hand over the monopoly on force to the spooks. It had been a bitter pill to swallow, but the alternative was to see the dream die. Building a new nation from the ground up was an exercise in compromise. The Mob, of course, had a similar seat in the presidential cabinet, one that wielded a thermonuclear-class national monopoly. The secretary of the national interest made every other detail of life on the platform his personal interest. The drug manufacturing, import-export regulations, exchange rates on foreign currency, gambling, girls and restaurateuring were all within the absolute jurisdiction of the national interest.

Which left Cassandra with the administrative details. He was a front man, plain and simple. When the alliance needed a man to talk to the cameras and issue a sound bite, he was their talking head. Less a president and more of a bag boy for the real powers that had all but coopted his dream.

In his own mind, it was time for a change. It would have to be a quiet coup. Nothing loud and violent that would disturb his suitors. His biggest obstacle was the CIA. No doubt about that. The spooks would always insist on keeping one of their own close to the operation. That wasn't the problem. The problem was that their man was a true believer in the Company, as close to a diehard loyalist to the CIA as any covert operative could get. Cassandra needed a Company man with flexibility.

The necessity of bringing wise guy soldiers onto the platform to act as reinforcements was redundant at best. The current security detail could handle any task of mayhem at least as well as any Army infantry unit. It was the fact that they would back Dandridge in a hard play that gave him pause.

Ideologically, the wise guys were more resonant and open to Cassandra's vision than the Company would ever be.

Yes, the Mafia was composed of men that Damien Cassandra could deal with and speak to in a language that cut through all the bullshit. They had a huge stake in the success of Cassiopeia, and therefore marshalling troops to provide for the common defense was to be expected. Dandridge hadn't even raised an eyebrow when the wise guys wanted to bring in their own specialists. Well, hell, it was a partnership, right?

Damien Cassandra had been around the block a time or two.

His office was located on level two, in the government wing. He had a corner office facing to the northeast, and the two outside walls were made of reinforced glass.

From where he was standing, the yacht was like a small-scale model in the gray-blue ocean. He had watched the dinghy come ashore unmolested. He had thought about what that might mean. He had to assume that whatever was lurking in the waters off Cassiopeia had to have come from down deep. Where there was no light. Ever. During the day, the monsters had to stay down deep. Sure, that had to be it. When it got dark, the creatures came up to the surface in search of food.

He was already seeing the glimmer of a possibility— shift export ops to daylight hours only. Strangle the easy food supply. Maybe the bastards would move on. Those experts that were onboard now should be able to give him an idea of how long it would take to starve the beasts out.

The speakerphone on his desk beeped. It was Amanda, his executive assistant, in the front office. Whoever had come ashore from the yacht wanted an audience. Cassandra was anticipating that.

"Mr. Cassandra, there is—"

"Yes, Amanda. I know. Show them in, please."

A moment later the door into his office opened. Amanda stepped through and stood to one side.

"Mr. Cassandra, this is Mr. Wesson Fairchild and party from the Bermuda Conservatory," she said.

Amanda was a looker, but the two women who flanked Fairchild into the office were the kind of beautiful that was dangerous. The women both had the hypnotic eye contact of a cobra, the sexuality of an incubus and the presence of a black widow spider. The blonde was wearing a white cocktail dress with spaghetti straps. The brunette had on an identical dress that was the same shade of red as arterial blood. Their straggler seemed out of place in both dress and personal presence. He seemed furtive and spooked. Cassandra took in the conservative suit, trench coat and leather briefcase. This guy was definitely hired help. Cassandra pegged him as being the accountant or lawyer.

"Thank you, Amanda," Cassandra said. "That will be all."

He waited for her to close the door.

Cassandra went on, "If you are here to litigate over the tragic loss of life and property two nights ago, don't bother. Your lawsuits mean nothing here. Cassiopeia is a sovereign state with no extradition treaties. We are not liable for what amounts to an act of God in our waters."

Damien Cassandra was a master of reading his fellow humans. To swim with sharks, you had to be able to communicate with the sharks. Cassandra knew a bad news bear when he saw one. Wesson Fairchild didn't wear a priest's black suit with a black collar just because he was trying to be a walking statement. That collar was exactly right for Wesson Fairchild. It was exactly who he was.

Cassandra knew these things and more in an instant, a flash of impressions riffling his mind.

Fairchild's voice was low-key when he spoke.

"What is taking place here is exactly that—an act of God. But let's be clear on which god it is we're talking about here. The religion I represent, Mr. Cassandra, was old when this world was still a molten rock in space. When you say God, Mr. Cassandra, I conceptualize something entirely different than the Judeo-Christian God you are conditioned to define the term by. Jesus and Jehovah have nothing to do with your problems out here."

Cassandra paced along the glass wall facing the anchored yacht. The exact nature of the hostile marine life plaguing Cassiopeian waters had yet to be given a name. It had to be something like giant sea snakes or giant octopuses.

"Are you suggesting that you might have something to do with this problem?"

"I am connected to these events, Mr. Cassandra, in the same way a butterfly's wings fluttering are connected to the birth of a killer hurricane on the other side of the world."

"Chaos theory." Cassandra acknowledged the reference the black priest was making.

"We call it magick."

"Whatever, but back to my problem. So you've put a curse on my little republic, called up some godforsaken monster from Hell and turned it loose on us. Is that the drift I'm getting here?"

"I'm sending you no drift."

"You came out here to let me in on something, right?"

Those black chocolate eyes narrowed.

"That would be a good way of putting it, yes."

"Okay, Wesson. Let me in on it already. I do have a country in a crisis to run."

"It would be best if you and your people abandoned your claims to these waters and to this structure you've built to celebrate vice. Leave right now, and nobody else has to die."

"Is that a threat?"

"No, Mr. Cassandra. It is prophecy."

Cassandra knew that he wasn't negotiating a merger here, dealing with another man across the table who was trying to get as much bang for his buck as Cassandra was for his. There weren't etiquette guidelines for what the two men were rolling up their sleeves to negotiate. Cassandra was genuinely being offered a choice that would lead to seeing tomorrow's sunrise on the one hand or to an unimaginable death on the other. Somehow, in some inexplicable way, Wesson Fairchild and those monsters of the deep that were hovering somewhere out there were intimately connected.

At any rate, the man deserved respect.

Cassandra spread his hands in a conciliatory gesture. "Is it okay if I call you Wesson, sir?"

Cassandra could see that his opponent favorably received tagging that "sir" on the end of the question.

"Yes, I appreciate the courtesy."

"Wesson, I listen to my guts. They've seldom been wrong. My guts are screaming bloody murder over what you're asking. Not so much that it pisses me off, but that my guts believe everything you are saying or suggesting."

"You seem to have a rare intuition. You are a natural channel."

"While my intuition tells me you're telling the truth, my logical, rational self doesn't buy it. Do you know the investment I have in this nation? You're asking me to walk away from my only real reason for living. Can you appreciate that?"

"Either choice you make will succeed in getting you out of our way."

His intuition was seldom wrong. But it was his life's work on the table here. Stick with it and die or walk away and live. His guts were warring over the question.

"We still have a lot of people out here. Even with the helicopters, it will take some time."

"My yacht stands ready to be a ferry boat."

"That's very generous."

"I see and feel your conflict in this matter. I even sympathize with it on some levels. But a prophecy from before the blackest aeons of time is coming to pass right here, right now."

Decision making needed timely information for the right choice to be made. Cassandra's mind was screaming for more information.

"What is it out there, Wesson? What kind of animal is that?"

"It's not one but many. It is the rarest and most fearsome predator Nature has ever produced. The proper human name for the avatar, I believe, is *Architeuthis dux*. We worship *Architeuthis* in the same way Catholics revere the Pope. This animal is divine and is our earthly liaison to our god in a physical form."

"But what is it? Some kind of giant octopus?"

Wesson Fairchild chuckled. "No. These creatures are squid. Giant squid."

A hunter-killer pack of giant squid was being directed by the avatar squid that was being remote controlled from the great beyond by a monster god looking to insinuate itself back into the real world. That about

The Gold Eagle Reader Service™ — Here's how it works:

Accepting your 2 free books and gift places you under no obligation to buy anything. You may keep the books and gift and return the shipping statement marked "cancel." If you do not cancel, about a month later we'll send you 6 additional novels and bill you just $26.70* — that's a saving of 15% off the cover price of all 6 books! And there's no extra charge for shipping! You may cancel at any time, but if you choose to continue, every other month we'll send you 6 more books, which you may either purchase at the discount price or return to us and cancel your subscription.

*Terms and prices subject to change without notice. Sales tax applicable in N.Y. Canadian residents will be charged applicable provincial taxes and GST.

GET FREE BOOKS and a FREE GIFT
WHEN YOU PLAY THE...

Just scratch off the silver box with a coin. Then check below to see the gifts you get!

SLOT MACHINE GAME!

summed up the gist of this scorecard. Cassandra's rational mind was reeling in utter disbelief, but he was still buying it all. The story wasn't preposterous at all.

Fairchild said with low paternal tones, "I can see you are a logical man living in a logical world. Logical minds need the concrete proof of the five senses, don't they? Perhaps a demonstration will help resolve this conflict of conscience for you."

He didn't wave his hand dramatically or chant something from an arcane spell book written in a demonic tongue. He stood there and smiled. When the first shotgun boomed beneath his feet and then all at once fifty or sixty soldiers were unloading with everything they had, Cassandra knew that the nightmare was back.

"What the fuck is going on?"

"A demonstration. You must see it to believe it. That's the point of a demonstration, right? Stay close to me and no harm will come to you. You have my word."

The squirrelly looking attorney or accountant took that suggestion to heart and became human flypaper on Fairchild. Fairchild laughed mockingly and the hired hand backed up.

"Relax, Morty. You still have juice with this organization." He looked across the big office to where Cassandra was still standing. "Morty thinks that we're going to feed him to something when his services are no longer needed. He's always so twitchy."

Cassandra said, "I sympathize with Morty."

Fairchild cocked his head toward the office door. The man seemed to be alight with a playful spirit, like a kid at show-and-tell. "Coming? This is the only proof you'll accept. Men like you must see it to believe it, right? I guarantee that you've never seen anything like this."

Cassandra had no doubt about that. He stepped away from the wall of glass as Fairchild turned and went for the doorknob, flanked by his women. The nervous guy stayed within ten feet of Fairchild after leaving the office. Cassandra parted the women to walk side by side with the black priest. In a different world using different tools, Damien Cassandra was as much a man of power as Wesson Fairchild was.

Whatever his decision was going to be, he'd be damned if he was going to make it on any other footing but equal footing, squared off and shoulder to shoulder. He would never walk in the shadow of this man.

THE STUN GUNS hadn't knocked Mack Bolan completely unconscious. He was in a quasi-dream state and his limbs were seized up, refusing to take any direction at all from the central nervous system. His eyes rolled under slit lids, wild and unfocused. His arms were taped together in front of him with duct tape, and he was dragged into the meat locker by two black-clad security troops. One of them circled his arms around Bolan's waist and lifted his body off the floor while a comrade looped his taped wrists over the metal hook in the ceiling. When he was let go, his body was completely suspended. If he pointed his toes, his boot tips would scrape the metal deck.

His legs hadn't been bound. He needed to regain some motor control, fast. His thoughts seemed to be moving at the speed of cold oatmeal. His ears were still working properly, but the parts of his brain that were supposed to make sense of the signals were struggling to come back on line.

He'd taken quite a jolt. Five guys armed with one

300,000-volt Panther stun gun each. He'd absorbed several five-gun salutes and one or two or three discharges along with a kick to the ribs or face. These were the kind of men that liked it getting brutal when there was no chance of charges being filed, paperwork or investigations being done. A guy could really cut loose when he knew there would be no repercussions.

He heard a dream character walking in front of him and circling to his rear saying something that sounded like "Get Matt and Mark. Tell them to bring their turkey kits. I got a holiday bird just waiting for their special touch."

Those two words—turkey kits—sparked some basic survival override that could get a signal through all the nerve noise to his legs. Of all the ways that Mack Bolan could possibly die, this was the one death he would not tolerate to be forced upon him. He'd make them kill him first.

He heard the messenger dispatched, hitting the panic paddle that released the locking mechanism to the door from inside the freezer. The thick insulated door popped open with a kiss and the troop's boot heels made dull thuds on the tile as he jogged through the kitchen and out into the mezzanine to get Matt and Mark as directed.

The dream character turned out to be Link Dandridge. Bolan knew it was Link when his head was yanked backward by his hair and the mouth practically inside his ear was using Dandridge's voice.

"You know what a turkey is, boy? It's an old family tradition back in Jersey, where I'm from. You're gonna tell us everything you know."

He seemed to think that was funny.

When Dandridge got some of his composure back,

he punched Bolan in the right ear and let his head go. An explosion of noise and color and pain rocked his brain. He gritted his teeth but didn't cry out. His vision was clearing. His body was swinging back and forth on the meat hook bolted into the ceiling. The cold was starting to leach through his woolen shirt. He noticed that Dandridge was hugging himself.

Bolan was hooked and hanging with a side view of the door. The thick door was yanked open and held by the runner. Matt and Mark were each lugging a large leather suitcase that took a two-hand grip to move around.

Once inside the freezer, the suitcases hit the floor and the two of them began looking around with growing disgust.

Dandridge didn't have the time or the patience for their outrage. "Something not to your liking?"

"We need tables," Matt said.

"Yes," Mark echoed. "And not just any tables. We're doctors. I want stainless-steel cutting tables like you'd find in any good OR in any reputable hospital."

Dandridge couldn't believe his ears. "Does this look like a goddamn hospital? This is a meat locker in a freaking kitchen, okay?"

"Have you noticed how much we end up doing work in settings like this?" Matt said.

Mark wasn't sure if it was the wording of the question or the question itself. But it sparked something burning and hot.

"Yes. It's a redundancy that clearly reveals what they really think of us."

"We're butchers to them."

"Maybe it's because we're always put to work in a

sausage plant or slaughterhouse or meat packing warehouse."

"Yeah. Like we do our work on dead meat."

"Dead meat is for butchers."

"Living flesh is for artistes," Matt said.

The cold was becoming a good excuse to make an exit to look for acceptable tables. Dandridge bellowed, "Let's find these men some suitable tables!"

He straight-armed through the door and into the kitchen. His five security troops followed. Matt and Mark walked around to where Bolan could see them both without having to turn his head. The thick walls of the freezer muffled a cacophony of clattering bangs as stainless-steel cooking gear was swept off tabletops and the tables were dragged across the tiled floor.

Bolan was tensing his thighs and relaxing, testing his legs by muscle groupings for function. He tucked and lifted his knees. He wondered if he could put it all together into one coordinated action when the opportunity presented itself. He'd have to.

Matt and Mark had their arms crossed and were looking at the Executioner with the eyes of an artist gazing upon a block of virgin stone, imagining what would be carved into existence.

"He's a big one," Matt observed.

"He won't make it to the end of step one," Mark replied.

"Probably not. These big boys shatter the easiest. Everything else is icing."

The freezer door was jerked open and a stainless-steel table shoved into the cold storage by two troops. A second table rumbled in behind the first with two more security goons latched on for propulsion. The tables were left in the center of the freezer next to each other. Dandridge stalked back in and snarled, "There's your fucking tables."

Matt said, "Put them against that wall and get our bags up on top. Thanks."

Dandridge started chuckling and the chuckling became a gale of laughter. Suddenly, Dandridge wasn't laughing anymore. His face was deadpan and his eyes looked like cold fusion plutonium.

"We're paying your bill when a bill is presented. So set up your own fucking tables."

Mark didn't seem to like the way Dandridge was treating the two specialists.

"If you don't want to help us set up our tools, fine. But when we break a subject, we do it alone! You and your men can go back to whatever it was you were doing previously, and either Matt or I will come get you when you can start having your fun."

Dandridge looked at Bolan dangling there, so helpless. It gave him joy to see that rat bastard helpless at last.

"You just make sure that this takes a long time. That's the most important part of our agreement."

"Long time no problem," Mark said.

10

In the jargon of neurolinguistic programming, what Mallory Harmon had done to Brown Eyes was called anchoring.

She'd done a lot of different things to him quickly to get inside his defenses, but the thing with the elbow—that was called an anchor. She had elicited the desired state in him and then, when she had him at an emotional peak, she clutched his left arm at the elbow break and anchored the state to the touch. She continued saying the things that she knew he had craved to hear from a woman all his life and, at key points, squeezed his elbow and triggered the state again, reinforcing and maintaining the desired state. She wanted to keep him there.

She finessed him and kept his normal behavioral patterns toward attractive women lulled away, neurologically forgotten. Harmon was blessed with brains and good looks; she was exactly the kind of woman this guy would normally isolate and rape until she was barely alive. Then he would kill her. He'd dispose of her body with no more guilt than normal people felt about taking out the garbage. It was all part of his pattern. She'd

scrambled that pattern before it could build up dangerous pressure.

Now she was the one trying to isolate the prey.

She had been eyeing the big, lighted floor directories
with arrows that pointed up, down, right and left.

She needed to get this guy somewhere out of ear and
eyeshot. Harmon decided that level three, Admin & Ac-
commodations would offer numerous possibilities for
rendering him harmless. She was his rudder now. Where
Mallory Harmon steered this serial predator, he was
going to follow her willingly.

The stairwell to level three opened up through the
watertight bulkhead in the center of the near 800,000
square feet of floor space shared by three divisions.

She led him up the stairs with her arm looped through
his left arm at the elbow, and she had her free hand
lightly clutched there at the break, keeping that trigger
firing. Harmon was marveling at the power she wielded
right now, over a species of predator that wasn't normally thought of as being controllable.

She was using her voice like a psywar weapon. "Could
you hang out here, love, while I find us a place to, ah, talk?"

His face was blissful and blank.

"Yes," he said, hissing on the *S*. "Okay. Love."

She shuddered with the feeling he put into verbaliz-
ing that word, *love*. She smiled with every ounce of
warmth she could muster and fired the trigger again.

"Don't worry. I won't leave you."

She released his left arm and backed away slowly
without breaking eye contact. She smiled, and genuine
warmth was radiating off her body like solar flares. She
wasn't faking this now. She was horrified and incredulous

all at once that a side of her psyche seemed to know what this freak needed the most and wanted to provide it.

Why? Why not just put a 10 mm hole in the sicko's brainpan and end it all there?

Today, Dr. Mallory Harmon, Special Agent with the FBI's Behavioral Sciences Unit, was batting a thousand. Her theory was working right here and now, and that's all that really mattered. Right now, something to exploit.

She quickly scanned the mezzanine. She was center mass of the platform, and this was the hub. It was the only real open market on the planet. The government of Cassiopeia Republic had two booths on the mezzanine: the government services directory desk and the immigration desk. The immigration desk was always closed. There was a commodities brokerage where major traffickers made deals for product by the ton. The brokerage cubicles were closed as well. Then there was an area like a food court in a mall, but it was a drug court. There were armadas of kiosks and cappuccino buggies that sold amphetamines, cola and pure seedless hydrobuds in kilo sizes and under. It was the marketplace for the rave crowd—the party animals who wanted to keep rocking and rocking until severe mental collapse set in. Most of these dealerships were closed, but several were being staffed to serve the skeleton crew and contract defenders sent to keep the micronation intact through this weird crisis. Single hits of alertness aids like methamphetamine were on the house. Everything else was going for wholesale prices, thirty to fifty percent off what the loot would be going for if the bazaar was fully open for business. It was a way for Cassiopeia to say thank-you to her friends.

The scheduling desk for the escort services was paying overtime to the girls who decided to stay, and the Cassiopeian government was picking up the tab.

The hotel front desk was abandoned, and a Peg-Board was propped up in a plastic chair behind the desk. A third of the pegs still had room keys hanging, up for grabs. A handwritten sign in black marker letters stated: Please Take Only the Keys for the Rooms Being Used and Occupied. If the Room Isn't Being Used, Leave the Key so Someone Else Can Use It.

Harmon noticed a laminated floor plan of the lodging wing lying on the floor and she picked it up, looking for a room located in the most remote corner of the wing. She vaulted over the counter and began checking room numbers with available keys.

She was continuing to have one of those rare, hypercongruent days. When everything seems to just work out right.

The most remote suite in the corner of the platform facing due northwest was unoccupied. She plucked the key off the board and used the door this time to get back on the other side of the counter. She hurried back to the center of the mezzanine where she'd left her lab rat. But her lab rat was vectoring in on her like a shark to blood in the water. He didn't have that blissed-out look to his eyes anymore. Those brown eyes were whirlpools of the darkest passions. His teeth were showing through lips that could be called a smile or a snarl. Painted on *his* face, she knew that teeth showing meant he was in attack mode.

Her studies of Aikido kept her from completely panicking.

HARLAN GARRISON WAS packing to leave. He'd had enough. They'd been abusing every designer drug known to today's rave crazy youth—just as long as the drug in question could be snorted, swallowed or smoked in a crack pipe. Freaking needles were out, man. He'd been horrified of needles since he was a boy growing up in the coal mining hills of Kentucky, and nothing had changed in over fifty-six years. The lunatic reunion had been going on strong for almost seventy-two hours straight. Unbelievable. But the soundproof suite was paid for out of the very generous proceeds a group of former yippies turned Hollywood moguls had shelled out for the rights to make a righteous movie out of his classic novel of the dope decade.

The fact that he was a millionaire now didn't change the edgy lifestyle he'd invented and refined since the Summer of Love. The only difference now was that he really had the financial wherewithal to push the envelope beyond the boundaries of class and good taste.

He was trying to fit the lamp fixture from the bureau into one of his gigantic leather suitcases. He had three of the barge-sized bags open and haphazardly packed on top of the two double beds. The curtains were drawn and had been since the reunion went supernova almost three days ago. They still weren't aware in any concrete sense of the menace lurking in the waters below or of the massive carnage that had taken place two nights ago.

He tried to slam down the lid on his suitcase, but the lamp was too big. He couldn't get the zipper closed. With a growl, he jerked the lamp out and threw it against the wall. The ceramic base shattered with a crash. There was something about trashing hotel suites that soothed the wild beast. He felt better already.

He slammed the lid back down and zipped the suitcase closed. He repeated the operation with the other two bags on the other bed. He dragged the bags to the door and staged them there. There was no way he was going to get all the bags up to the flight deck by himself in one trip, and he was damned if he was going to make three trips by himself.

He needed some staff assistance. Fast.

Garrison jerked open the door to the soundproof suite and bellowed, "I need a bellhop! Now!"

His eyes widened at the sight on the other side of the door. It wasn't staff assistance jumping to his beck and call, no. A man had a woman pressed against the wall. Her arm was twisted behind her back, and he was using it like a lever, applying pain in direct proportion to the torque threatening to separate her socket from the shoulder. His free hand was filled with a big nasty black handgun, and the muzzle was buried into her disheveled strawberry-blond hair.

The sudden eruption of the door opening and Garrison's howl had to have scared the man with dark hair because he jumped, then whirled, pointing the large bore pistol into Garrison's face.

"What are you lookin' at? Get back in your room!"

Garrison screeched and backpedaled in retreat. The woman suddenly wasn't immobilized anymore. She became a fire-breathing wolverine with blood in her eyes. She pushed off the wall and pivoted while driving her open palm into the back of the man's head. She didn't hold anything back. The hand bone to head bone crack and instant swimming eyeballs graphically portrayed the power behind the blow. His body was thrown forward, lifted right out of his loafers and sent sailing into the open suite. A spasm of nerve noise jerked the trigger finger, and one thundering round went wide and wild, smacking into the wall where the corridor jogged back at a right angle toward the mezzanine.

Garrison and the enforcer went down inside the doorway in a tangle of limbs.

The H&K .45 SpecOps pistol hit the carpeting in the corridor, and Mallory Harmon snatched it up on her way into the suite right behind her opponent. The hammer was locked back ready to touch off round number two. She wasn't going to kill him unless his behavior left her no other choice. She was still a federal agent with a duty to observe the formalities of the rights of the accused. She wanted to see this one caged for future research on her part. She was determined to see if it could be done.

But that would have to wait for another time. Other things were more immediate. Like the fate of the enigmatic Colonel Pollock. She had to do everything she could right now to spring him from the jaws of death. He'd do the same for her if the situations were reversed, she was certain.

The crazed guy with wild hair, shorts and Acapulco shirt was frantic to get out from under the hardman, still unaware that the man was now disarmed and on the verge of unconsciousness.

"I'll say nothing to no one!" Garrison yelled. "I just need a bellhop!"

Harmon dropped to one knee and used the enforcer's left kidney to cushion the blow. The guy gasped, back arching, head flopped between contracting shoulder blades offering a perfect target. She clubbed him again. This time, she struck him behind the ear with the magazine butt. The sound of the impact was sharper, louder, carrying much more weight.

The Mob soldier went down. Garrison kicked off the

unconscious body and scrambled to his feet. Harmon rolled the guy onto his chest and jerked his hands behind his back. She looked at Garrison, recognition slowly coming to the surface of her slate-gray eyes.

"Got any shoelaces?" she asked.

"Uh-uh. I've got some clothesline."

"Hand it over."

Garrison began spastically uprooting trash and plates with half-eaten entrees and coconut husks in search of the clothesline.

"Clothesline…where did I put the clothesline?"

He went to the writing desk where beer cans and foam cups surrounded the vintage black IBM Selectric typewriter. A grapefruit was impaled to the desktop with a Bowie knife of Rambo proportions. He jerked the blade tip out of the wood and wielded the knife, grapefruit and all. He used it to root through the clutter.

Harmon pulled her undergarments out of the pockets of the downed man's blazer. She stuffed them in her cargo pockets and looked up. Garrison was staring at her, posing like a crane trying to take flight. She could see by the look on his face that he was going to ask.

"Don't ask," she growled.

Garrison went back to probing the unbelievable amount of refuse all over the suite with the knife. "Of course not," he muttered. "I'd never ask a thing like *that*."

Harmon scanned the room. The bathroom door was completely blocked from view by the tall wall locker and a taut cotton line extended from behind the locker, tied off to the sink faucet. A good ten feet of line was left trailing the tie-off job. She didn't ask why a clothesline was strung across the room, and Garrison didn't offer an explanation.

She stood and snapped, "Give me the knife."

He reversed his grip from the knife to the grapefruit and offered it to her. She pulled the knife free and stalked into the vanity area. She cut the clothesline off just behind the intricately tied knots and rolled it up. She returned the big knife to the grapefruit and quickly tied the hardman's hands behind his back. Then she ran the remaining line down to his ankles and tied them off, as well.

"You must have been a Brownie," he remarked.

"Nope. I used to be a dominatrix. But don't let that circulate, okay?" She smiled devilishly.

"Jesus God! And what do you do now?"

"I'm an FBI agent. Help me get him on the bed," she said.

Garrison complied.

After getting the unconscious enforcer onto one of the double beds, she stuck the .45 autoloader into her waistband and concealed the weapon under her vest.

"So, what's this guy going down for?"

"I believe he's a serial sex killer who happens to work for the Mafia."

"Why not just shoot the fucker like a dog right now?"

"Because I want to take him with me. Keep him in my dungeon, you know."

She smiled that smile again and winked on top of it.

"The Bureau really has gone completely sideways!"

"Listen, Mr. Garrison, if you help me, I'll help you. Do you want to get off this rig?"

Garrison did.

In spades.

11

Vince Ribaldi had been slowly making his way back up the stairs ever since Manny Baglio took the strangers up to meet the man of the house. At first, it was only two steps up from what was left of the floating dock sections. Lou Ventura stayed close to the tethered dinghy and passed the time by lighting up a cigarette. Every time he glanced back at Ribaldi, the man was one more step up from where he was before. If Ventura didn't say something soon, he knew the bastard would be calming his nerves at the bar with a frigging margarita.

He flicked the butt of his smoke over the cable railing and watched the stay-behind sitting in the dinghy. The guy matched stares with Ventura and smiled like something nocturnal and carnivorous. It was starting to make him mad. Ventura was this much away from drilling the prick right in that punk smile with the Benelli M-1. Instead, he leaned the shotgun against the cable rail and shook another cigarette out of the pack.

He lit up and glanced behind him. He had to look up now to see the full Vince. That bastard was halfway up the deck overhead. Ventura was disgusted. He wanted to shoulder the Benelli and save the Mob some face in the eyes of this outsider.

"Vince!" he boomed. "You're makin' our Family look like a bunch of assholes. I should blow you offa those stairs for that alone!"

"But I got a great view from up here, Lou! You know! In case that bastard tries something!"

"You've got five seconds to get back down here!"

"But, Lou—"

"Now, Vince!"

"Okay!"

The dock under his feet raised sharply and dropped. Ventura jerked around and grabbed for the cable railing. The punk in the dinghy was smiling with even more feral intensity. Just a wave, he thought. Just a fucking swell. His momentary loss of composure really sparked off his anger.

"If you don't stop lookin' at me like that, I'm gonna jump over this rail and kick your goddamn ass!"

He snatched up the Benelli shotgun and held it at the ready.

There was another disturbance in the water behind him in the distance, followed by a sound that was almost reminiscent of a scream or a call for help. But it was cut off too quickly to register positively as such. The aluminum planks under his deck shoes telegraphed the vibration of something bad like a giant guitar string. Ventura pivoted back toward the stairs.

Vince was gone. Ventura looked up higher. Nothing. The stairs seemed to be swaying gently as if something had reached up out of the water and swatted the rickety structure. And there was something else. An odor. Tingling faintly but growing more pronounced. He couldn't place it.

Somebody topside was yelling like hell.

"Hey! Hey! Did you see that? Did you see that fucking thing!"

Not an animal. A thing. A monster. Something right out of a nightmare. And Ventura knew that Vince had been right all along. They were in the wrong goddamn place. Nobody had any business being down here on the water—waters that were still choked with the drifting remnants of carnage beyond belief from two nights before. But what frosted him the most and spilled liquid ice through his bowels was the blinding realization that he was next.

He was the last in line, sure.

That punk in the dinghy was finally loosening his jaws and speaking.

His two cents' worth wasn't even worth that.

"Hey, tough guy. You're food for the avatar now."

Lou Ventura might be three heartbeats away from the big sleep, but he wasn't going to take any shit like this standing up. He was from Jersey for Christ's sake. He spun while shouldering the Benelli 12-gauge.

"Yeah? Well, so are you, dirtbag!"

With the shotgun, Ventura didn't have to worry about aiming. Just point the muzzle in the right direction and jerk the trigger. The weapon exploded like the end of the world and belched out a flaming package of combusting gases, disintegrating wadding and steel BBs. The man in the dinghy came apart from the chest up. It was beautiful in its sheer ugliness, no questions. The man's head, neck and shoulders were erased in a splash of crimson petals, like a blooming rose that was made of blood, bone and tissue. The solid remains of his body were catapulted off the rubber cell of the dinghy in the transfer of energy from muzzle-blast to target impact. The headless bleeding mess made a splash in the cold gray water ten feet from the stern of the rubber watercraft. The body was buoyant with air in the lungs and should have stayed afloat.

But something intervened.

Ventura saw something purple and thick loop up out of the water and encircle the dead torso like a constricting snake.

That stench was overpowering, but Ventura still couldn't define it. His eyes were watering, and breathing was almost impossible. The shotgun-shredded body of the coxswain was snatched beneath the surface with a violent yank. The only evidence that a human body had existed there was a swirling whirlpool of ocean stained cherry-red.

In the wake of that disappearance, the waters bowed and domed over something coming up from below. It was unimaginably huge. Ventura was saucer-eyed with horror looking down into the biggest eyeball he'd ever seen. It was as big around as a Mack-truck tire. Cradled in a jelly slime shaped like a gigantic torpedo that was the color of oxygen-starved blood. Man and alien life-form eyeballed each other across the distance of a dozen feet.

Ventura went instinctive.

The M-1 shotgun was an autoloader. Round two was just waiting for the word. He corrected his aim down and out, and squeezed the trigger again. Fire and iron balls reached out and touched that big eyeball, which disappeared in an eruption of pus. Ventura had the satisfaction of that before the final curtain fell.

Something hit him from behind, looping up over his head and clamping down with frightening power. The lights went out and he couldn't breathe, couldn't scream. He had the sensation of being lifted off his feet and lofted into the air as he struggled for breath. White-hot points, like a thousand ice picks, were puncturing his head, neck, shoulders and torso all at once. The Atlantic swallowed his body whole.

He died as his body was spun into bloody gruel and funneled down into the snapping, parrotlike beak of a monster that should have only existed in a horror movie.

The Benelli M-1 shotgun spiraled down into the gloom, the only grave marker he'd ever have.

JAKE LASSITER COULDN'T believe his eyes. His attention was jerked to the huge disaster-proof bay windows by the double blasts of a shotgun. He was on the upper lounge deck of level six when the shit hit the fan. Outside the massive glass slabs, the polymer treated wood planks of the wraparound deck were exploding from below, and bullwhipping tentacles as big around as baby redwoods were lashing and snaring screaming hardguys, jerking the thrashing bodies into the waters below. Those clear of the breaches were running for the solid sanctuary of reinforced concrete and steel inside the bar. Several brave hearts were standing their ground and unleashing blistering autofire into the churning waters.

Dante couldn't have put a more horrific scene into epic words of poetic power. It was straight out of Hell.

The bedlam outside on the deck instantly turned the interior into a command and control nightmare.

The street soldiers were following the cues from their own organic hierarchies or just plain going cowboy on their own. The undisputed alpha males in each Family clique were barking orders at their own boys and at one another, trying to take the reins and put one voice in command of all the others. It didn't work out at all. Nobody perceived as being a leader wanted to step aside and give it all up to one unified commander. So nobody was in command. And everybody was armed to the teeth with pistols, machine guns and military ordnance.

Lassiter looked around, goggle-eyed at the staged chaos unfolding, and tried to lock on to something he could positively control. He saw the women, the dancers, cowering on their raised stages hugging their fire poles, wild-eyed with fear and looking for a savior.

He erupted into action.

"Get these women out of here!" he yelled.

He grabbed a soldier by the ballistic nylon of his assault vest and yanked him around.

"Get your men together, goddammit, and get these women the hell off this deck! Now!"

GUIDO TANTARELLA continued to layer sliced roast beef onto a sandwich that was already three and going on four inches thick. The complete loss of control all around him didn't deter his building of a genuine triple-decker. He was now the only man left standing at the sandwich bar.

Lon Holmberg, one of his loyal shooters, skidded into the bar with a thump right next to him, wide-eyed and breathless.

"Guns ain't stoppin' those things whatever they are, boss!"

"Did we or did we not bring along a crate or two of hand grenades?"

"Yeah, but they said no bombs!"

"I don't care what they said. Drop a few of those jewels into the water, and those bastards will take note.

They're animals, Lon. Like all things in the natural order, they understand superior firepower. Get it?"

"But—"

"Are we here to do a job or what? Drop the grenades, and we're out of here by nightfall."

"But—"

Tantarella put his plate down and gave Holmberg the dead-eye stare. It was the kind of look that spelled *fish bait* if compliance wasn't granted immediately. Holmberg knew he'd said too much already and put a clamp on it.

"Okay, boss. I'll tell the boys to drop a few bombs, and we're takin' care of business."

"That's right, Lon. We're taking care of business here and business is good."

Tantarella palmed the plate again. Holmberg pushed off the bar to relay the word, and the big boss man decided that ranch dressing would be the perfect taste enhancement to the stacked masterpiece on his plate before adding the roofing slice of bread to finish off the manwich.

IT WAS the smartest thing Donovan West could think of doing once the bullets started flying. He threw their bags on the floor at his feet and flipped the table on its side to act as a shield. Then he was attacking her bag because he knew that she was packing heat.

Donovan West was James Bond in his own mind but when the shit hit the fan, he didn't have a damned clue as to how to save his own ass let alone anyone else's. Since he was unarmed in an armed camp, the best bet was to get his fingers wrapped around a piece. And then just wing it from there.

He wondered what Mallory would do right now as

he frantically dug through her belongings looking for the pistol. Whatever he thought of the woman personally was immaterial. The fact was, she knew how to stay cool in a hot situation. And she knew how to shoot like a demon, too.

His fingers brushed supple leather hugging hard, cold steel. The pistol. He yanked the holstered weapon out of the depths of her extra clothing and pulled it free of leather. He flipped the black handgun back and forth in his hands, checking out both sides of the slide. The safety was on. He unlocked the weapon and decided to make sure that there was a round ready to fire. He pulled the slide back, and the round in the pipe ejected.

Goddammit. Of course the weapon was ready to fire. She wouldn't carry it any other way.

He scrabbled to catch the skittering round as it bounced around the floor like a Mexican jumping bean.

James Bond, damn straight.

LON HOLMBERG disengaged the latches on the OD green crate and flipped the lid open. Inside were a dozen cardboard canisters, each holding a single M-33 "baseball" fragmentation grenade.

He told his boys from the Yonkers contingent, "Everybody take one."

"But, Lon, they said no explosives, right?" Jimmy "Jinx" Tatagglia said.

Holmberg tried to duplicate his boss's death stare, but it didn't quite stack up.

"Guido says to hell with them. Just grab one, pull the pin and drop the bomb over the edge. We'll all be home by dinnertime."

"You sure?"

"For cryin' out loud, Jinx! Just do what I say, okay?"

Six of the seven soldiers eagerly grabbed a canister, ripped the seal and lid off and dropped the OD green metal bombs into their palms like kids with cherry bombs. Holmberg had to force one on Tatagglia, who held the grenade as if it might go off on its own if he breathed too hard.

Holmberg took a canister for himself, peeled it open and plopped the grenade into his hands.

"Okay. Pick a side and let's do it."

MALLORY HARMON BOUNDED down the main staircase from the casino to the lounge and pulled the .45 auto from under her vest. Half-naked strippers were running up the stairs in a panic, herded like cattle by five of the black-clad shooters. Nobody even gave her a second glance in the pandemonium. She hit the bottom of the stairs and pivoted toward the kitchen, but Link Dandridge and his five troops were bursting through the swing double doors like human cannonballs and she backpedaled, plowing into Garrison hot on her heels.

"Back up! Back up!" she exclaimed.

All she needed right now was to be spotted by that son of a bitch.

THE TWO TURKEY DOCTORS were obviously brothers. Both considered themselves as artistes, not sadistic butchers. The two had distilled their craft into a formula, a step-by-step process of escalating trauma to the physical organism, which in turn shredded a mark's psyche. They flirted with death, teased with the promise of that ultimate release but never let the mark get to that plateau. They constantly kept the mark on the brink of death but chased the reaper away with blood transfusions, electric shock, adrenaline injections—whatever it took to keep the mark alive, breathing and above all else—conscious of what was being done to his body.

Death couldn't be staved off forever. Death was always the final step.

The man named Matt was circling to Bolan's front, his hands filled with chains and leg manacles. Bolan sensed movement behind him, stalking in close.

Time to fight.

Bolan didn't even think about what to do. His legs were free and Matt was right in front of him. The knowledge of what step one was going to entail did wonders for his recovery time. He snapped his knees to his chest and scissored his legs around Matt's head. He simultaneously heaved his chest upward, using his leg lock on Matt as leverage, and flung his bound wrists up and over the meat hook he was dangling from.

The Executioner was free.

Bolan reached for the floor as his torso dropped like a pendulum into Matt's thighs, shoulder blades cracking into knees. The soldier's body mass knocked the turkey doctor's feet out from under him, and Bolan yanked his knees into his chest again as he flipped, bringing Matt along for the ride. The guy's head traded places with his shoes, and Bolan's knees smashed against the cold metal floor painfully with the torturer's head still locked firmly between his thighs.

The Executioner was rewarded with the sickening snapping pop of head bone fracturing and neck vertebrae violently compressing into bone shards and pulped nerve cord. Matt was dead in midsomersault as the rest of him came crashing back to the floor, legs kicking wildly in dying nerve firings.

Bolan rolled left and bounded up.

Mark was gaping in genuine shock at this ugly reversal. His mouth was moving, but no words were coming out. Just gurgles.

Bolan grinned with feral hatred and said, "Excellent final words, punk."

He rushed the stunned turkey doctor and coldcocked the guy with clasped hands. Mark flew into stacked boxes of frozen meat and thrashed. Bolan continued his forward rush and kicked the panic paddle on the door with his full weight behind the blow. He bolted into the kitchen as the heavy door crashed into the stainless-steel skin of the insulated wall and rebounded.

The Desert Eagle .50 AE was where Dandridge had left it, on a cutting table with the rest of his gear. He scooped up the heavy cannon in a two-handed grip and flicked off the safety with a thumb. The freezer door crashed open again behind him, and Bolan dropped into a combat crouch while pivoting. A handgun boomed, but the bullet meant for the Executioner's back cut the air harmlessly overhead.

Now it was Bolan's turn.

He wasn't normally a passionate killer, but the circumstances of this scene weren't normal. He needed this kill. It was very, very personal. It was a snap shot aimed on instinct and blood lust alone. The .50-caliber round going off in the confines of the kitchen was like concentrated Doom, pure fire and noise. The recoil was vicious; the muzzle climbed up almost ninety degrees before Bolan could bring it back down for another shot.

Not that his target needed a second bullet.

Bolan was known for taking head shots whenever possible. A head shot here just didn't seem like it would do this crime justice. Bolan took the gut shot, plain and simple. That 500-grain bullet sailing in at greater than the speed of sound made a gory demonstration of the physics of gunfire. The guy's hips blew apart like a balloon full of blood and viscera. It was as if an invisible wrecking ball folded the guy in two at the waistline and pitched the mangled body back into the freezer with the rest of the meat.

Bolan stalked forward and shouldered around the door before it could close. He used his foot as a doorstop and stood on the threshold, admiring his handiwork. Blood was dripping from the ceiling, running down the walls and washing down the floor. What was left of the turkey doctor was lying face up in a crushed pile of boxes. His head was lolling back and forth, and his eyes weren't focusing on anything. The guy was still alive.

Bolan fired again and the dying human monster's head disintegrated. The .44 Desert Eagle would have left a neck stump and maybe part of the jaw behind. The .50-caliber version blew everything away.

Bolan regretted that he didn't have an expert rifleman's badge to leave conspicuously displayed in the middle of this carnage to sign his name to the deed.

The Executioner was here, boys.

HARMON MADE a quick observation while counting off heartbeats before peeking back around the corner at the foot of the stairs again. The main stairwell was a trapezoid that went straight up the center core of the environmental sandwich, and it seemed very open and airy. But at the first sign of a waterborne disaster, blast

doors on each level would drop down out of the open
bulkheads and hold back the cold Atlantic. The sea
level would have to rise over fifty feet for the upper
half of level six to be in danger of being submerged.
She filed that information away for future use. She
wondered if the internal sensors could be tricked into
dropping those slabs of vault-grade steel. It was the
kind of information that might come in very handy
down the road here.

She took a look.

Dandridge was acting like some kind of General Pat-
ton on Benzedrine and acid. He was barking disrespect-
ful ethnic slurs like a sadistic drill sergeant in total control.

He reiterated the need to keep from bombing the harbor, ending with "you stupid wop dago bastards!"

And then the harbor started to blow up, and one of
those "dago bastards" put a ham-sized fist into Dandridge's big mouth like a human hammer drill.

"Let's go," she said calmly.

She wanted to kiss Dandridge for the diversion as she
flowed around the corner.

TIP ZAPPOLO was two steps away from getting into the
lounge when the deck planks inches behind his heels
fragmented and were pulled away. There was a whistle
of air behind him and then a battering ram slammed into
his back. The energy of the blow transferred around his
body to his chest and back again.

Zappolo's arms were free, and he dug his fingers
into the door frame in a frantic bid to stay on the deck.
A monstrous, stinking purple-black tentacle was
wrapped around his chest. It was as big around as a full-

grown anaconda. The tentacle clamped down tighter, constricting his body like an anaconda, too.

He had air in his lungs and uttered a scream, high-pitched with fear.

The sudden blood pressure in his head was frightening. It felt as if his cheeks and forehead were going to split open any second. A phalanx of wise guys came to his aid, grabbing on to him and the tentacle, keeping the foul appendage from taking the man into the water. The rest of the mobsters ringed the breach in the deck and rained hot lead at the floating beast below.

Marty DiCaprio from the Yonkers contingent ran out on the deck and hooked back around to assist. Two other Yonkers boys bolted for the railing, pitching small metal balls that were both shedding a sliver.

"Stand clear! Stand clear!" DiCaprio yelled.

He jerked the pin from the hand grenade and flung the little bomb into the breach in the deck. Two explosive pops sent water geysers into the air about thirty yards west of Zappolo's monster attacker and then Di-Caprio's jewel exploded on contact with slime, flinging fetid chunks of flesh away from the greasy flash. Four more explosions echoed from the opposite side of the lounge, in the waters below the deck. DiCaprio's blast blew off the tentacle that was a second away from reducing Zappolo's chest size from 40 to a 10. Two guys wrestling with it felt it relax and quickly peeled it off the man while the third guy dragged him into the lounge. The tentacle dropped back into the waters stained with alien blood.

Then Tatagglia hit the deck, cupping the grenade in both hands like a hot potato. He pulled out the pin and flung the bomb toward the railing. The treated cedar planks in front of him exploded from below, and the whip arm of another killer squid lofted through. The grenade was deflected like a lethal Ping-Pong ball, and Tatagglia was seized and jerked through the hole in the blink of an eye. He yelped on the way down, there was a terrific splash and then he was gone.

The grenade hit the six-inch-thick glass port just left of the big arched doorway into the lounge. It exploded on contact, destroying half of the floor-to-ceiling picture window in the blast. Solid sickles of glass razored into the lounge, flaying ten unfortunates who were too close to the big window. More of the deck was blasted away, raining smoking wood chunks into the thrashing, deadly waters.

USS Seawolf

GADGETS SCHWARZ WAS standing behind the *Seawolf*'s best sonar man, an enlisted guy named Bill Markle. The sonar man had his headphones on and was watching the luminous screen in front of him. He grabbed the mike off the console and keyed it.

"Conn, sonar! I have a huge contact in the water around the target! Dead ahead!"

The captain's voice boomed over the speaker, "Sonar, conn. Can you identify the contact?"

Markle was listening to the sounds in the water. Strange, frightening sounds.

"Conn, sonar. It's a marine animal of some kind. A lot of them. Probably hundreds!"

Another heartbeat and Markle really got excited. "Conn, sonar! I have exploding ordnance in the water!

Eight detonations—probably hand grenades… Small-arms fire—lots of it. The target is under attack, sir!"

Captain Chance remained impartial. "Thank you, Mr. Markle. I want immediate updates as the situation develops."

The captain's voice went to the one MC mode and was piped into every space, every hold aboard the *Seawolf.* "All hands, this is the captain. Battle stations. I say again—battle stations."

Schwarz tapped the sonar man urgently on the shoulder.

"Hey! Hey, take your phones off!"

Markle removed his phones and looked back at the Able Team commando.

"What is it, sir?"

"Hey, you've got training tapes, right? With underwater sounds? So you boys can train the newbies to better hone their skills? Identify organics from possible enemy sub contacts?"

Markle frowned and nodded. He didn't see what possible bearing that had on the current situation.

"Why? We're at battle stations, sir."

"So you've got a collection of whale calls, right?"

Markle nodded. The light still wasn't coming on.

Schwarz did, in fact, consider the condition of battle stations a very serious one. What Markle didn't understand was that Schwarz was assembling a weapon himself—a very potent one if staged properly.

"What about a sperm whale?" Schwarz asked, getting right down to brass tacks. "Better yet—a whole pod of sperm whales. You got anything like that on CD?"

"Yeah. We do." Markle was really frowning and taking second looks at the black-clad commando.

"Well, cue it up! I want you to broadcast the sperm whale calls on continuous play into the water in front of us. At full volume! Can you do that? At the same time, I want you to begin pinging the hell out of that contact with active sonar. Can you make that happen?"

"Why?"

"I don't have time to explain. But I think we'll disperse that pack real damn quick if you do what I say."

"I'll have to run this by the captain."

"By all means! Keep the chain of command informed!"

CAPTAIN NICK CHANCE had service-short black hair and murky green eyes. He looked more a man of twenty-six than thirty-three. He was an inch or two under six feet tall, lithe but not skinny. He was stout but not big. And the man was definitely in command here.

"Explain yourself, Mr. Schwarz."

"I want you to beam the recorded sounds of sperm whales into the water in front of us while actively pinging the sonar target at the same time. If I'm right, those things will haul ass for the deep, deep blue."

"Why sperm whales?"

"Sperm whales are its only known natural predator. Doesn't the Navy have a policy for these things?"

"We've never needed one. I don't like being left out of the information loop."

"You're about to cruise your boat through several million cubic feet of ocean infested with giant squid. If we make them think that this submarine is actually an intercepting sperm whale pod, I think they'll scatter. At least long enough to put the teams on the surface."

The captain's stern features relaxed and broke out in a smile.

"I like the way you think, Mr. Schwarz. In your dim past, you must have been a submariner."

Schwarz grinned.

The Cassiopeia Platform

BOLAN'S LST-5C satcom transceiver wasn't Army issue. The Army-Special Ops version needed the antenna packs designed for the radio or traffic would never be sent. Bolan still possessed the antenna packs, but to use the issue equipment would mean relocating to an open balcony or back to the flight deck. He'd need to have access to the sky to use the radio as issued.

Schwarz had modified the radio set. Now Bolan could hook into any coaxial cable and use its signal grid to route a message back to Stony Man Farm.

The kitchen was furnished with a color TV mounted to the ceiling. Bolan knew that the only TV this place would get was satellite broadcast. All the tubes on the platform were cabled into the same dish antenna. He cabled his radio into the kitchen TV feed and activated the dish-targeting program.

Bolan entered the coordinates for the covert bird.

He heard somebody coming through the double kitchen doors—spring-loaded flappers that a ninja couldn't stealth through. He palmed the huge Desert Eagle in his left hand while peeling left and going low.

Special Agent Mallory Harmon and the Executioner found themselves staring at each other over hair-triggers. A second figure blundered through the doors behind her, colliding into her as she dropped the barrel of her weapon.

Bolan recognized the guy's spastic body language and assaulting taste in attire. He wondered what trickster god it was that conspired to weave their paths together again. Bolan stood while lowering his weapon as well.

Harmon was studying Bolan and the general condition of the kitchen for clues.

"Well," she said, "I don't know why I was in such a hurry to get back here. Of course you would have everything buttoned up neatly."

Garrison peeked up over her shoulder and asked, "Who's that big bastard?"

"Somebody I thought needed some backup."

USS Seawolf

THE SLEEK, BLACK nuclear attack submarine was staying shallow at periscope depth. The antenna mast was up and monitoring the Stony Man covert communications satellite lurking at a classified right angle in the sky to the North Star. When Bolan sent his traffic, the sub intercepted it.

Schwarz was monitoring the frequency from sonar over the loudspeaker.

He snatched up the mike and stepped on the signal before Stony Man could reply.

He said, "This is cavalry chief to secret agent man Devlin Devereau. How copy, Devereau, over?"

The Cassiopeia Platform

BOLAN'S EYES narrowed.

"What's your twenty?" he snapped.

Harmon swallowed hard to banish the chuckles. She

was curious now about the two monster-sized men with suitcases she'd seen escorted in here to loosen Bolan's tongue. What had he done to them? The colonel's handgun was obscenely big bore. Her forensics curiosity was piqued.

She moved toward the freezer door.

"It's a bad scene in there," Bolan said. "Maybe you should skip it."

"Thanks for the advice," she replied and pulled open the insulated door. The soldier was right. It was a very bad scene in there. She went in anyway. After forty-seven autopsies now, performed under her own scalpel, Harmon was way beyond being squeamish in the face of extremely violent death. She identified the flavor of what had transpired in this little space with almost no effort on her part. It was like reading a picture book.

She felt an enormous amount of empathy for Bolan. She spun on her heel and got out of there.

Schwarz was cackling on his end.

"We're steaming into Little Amsterdam at periscope depth. Looks like a real obstacle course dead ahead on sonar."

"That's a serious obstacle course if you don't have a plan."

"I've got a plan, Striker. You know me, right? I'll be up with the rest of the team and a squad of SEALs as backup before you know it. Don't panic, Dev. We're here for you, buddy."

Bolan growled, "I'm looking forward to seeing you again, too. We'll prep the DZ for you. Striker out."

He began to disassemble the compact commo suite and Harmon seemed to materialize at his side like smoke. He had to admit—this woman had some moves. She touched his forearm very gently and said, "If you ever need some-body to talk to about this, I'm there to help you."

Bolan had to stop what he was doing and think about what she had just said to him. Then it hit him. This woman read crime scenes for a living. So he had to be very sure that she didn't go away from this with the wrong impression. He turned to face her and looked her square in the eyes. He gripped her shoulders firmly without being threatening.

"Listen, you've read it all wrong. That didn't go down. I got the drop on them before it could get that ugly."

He watched her eyes to make sure she understood and believed him. And was reminded of something the for-mer President had told him in the middle of a very strange scene. He repeated that truism for Harmon's sake.

"Sometimes you get the bear and sometimes the bear gets you."

She was studying his eyes for evidence of falsehood or deception. She saw none of that in his eyes. The fires were all still there in his icy blues…a little hotter maybe, a little angrier than she recalled from her last encounter with this man. She didn't see a tough guy facade trying to hide a huge bleeding hole in his soul.

As always, the colonel was straight as an arrow with his allies.

Harmon smiled with genuine relief.

"Don't worry about how angry you feel and what it made you do in there. I would have blown the bas-tards away, too."

Garrison had been doing an admirable job of keep-ing quiet in the corner and finding things of great interest in the ceiling tiles. Until Harmon made the comment about blowing the bastards away. It was just too horrible an image. He couldn't help physically reacting to it.

His jerky backpedals collided into a butcher block on wheels that smacked loudly into the wall and scattered utensils on the floor.

Harmon looked over at him with eyes that brought the curtain down on his production.

"Oh, get a grip, Garrison! We still have a lot of wood to chop here."

Harmon's admonishing tone flicked Garrison's switches. Panic mode was off, but sheer bravado mode was now on. Either way, it could still spell disaster.

"You're absolutely right, you perverted witch! We still have to hack our way through a room full of bull elk psychos. I must arm myself as well!"

Garrison knifed his hand into the hip pocket on his green shorts. His hand pulled out clutching the purse-sized can of pepper spray. It was his favorite method of self-protection.

Bolan watched Garrison in action without comment. He asked Harmon, "Do you have positive control on this guy?"

"Oh, sure. He's a teddy bear. He's candy, okay? Trust me, Colonel. What's the next play?"

From the sounds of the melee on the other side of the kitchen wall, Bolan knew that nobody had a grip on things in there.

"We're going to go out there and take charge."

12

The creatures were probably on the highest order of intelligence of anything lurking in the depths. The biggest brain nerve fibers of any animal known to science was encased inside the rubbery mantle that made up the head and body of the giant squid. They were pack hunters in the eternal darkness of the ocean two miles deep. But never had so many of their kind been gathered together like this in the collective memory of the species.

But never had there been one of their kind like the One.

It was bigger, faster and blacker than evil.

It stayed deep, in a gloom that was almost lightless. It was most comfortable in the borderlands between the ocean above and the ocean below. Very few things crossed the boundaries between the watery worlds and could reign supreme in either realm.

Architeuthis dux was one such creature.

The other creature big enough and brave enough to hunt *Architeuthis* in the dark wasn't a fish or an invertebrate. Just as man was the dominant mammal on land, in the oceans mammals were also at the top of the food chain and evolutionary ladders. The cetaceans were the monarchs of the open seas.

The great whales.

Of all the great whales, only the sperm whale seemed to harbor what could be viewed as an interspecies state of warfare with another denizen of the deep. Whales as a whole were highly intelligent and emotional mammals. The big sperms obviously had a good reason to risk the incredible water pressures, the darkness and an alien sentience to take down one of the monster squid when their natural soundings revealed one of the beasts below.

Science assumed that the sperm whale attacked giant squid because the huge mammals had acquired a taste for the ammonium-saturated flesh of these beasts. This feud between sperm whales and giant squid was purely a culinary pursuit. That was the scientific consensus on the subject.

The notion that the big sperms were killing the squid because the squid represented some kind of underwater threat on a planetary level had never been raised for serious debate.

Man had hunted the big sperm whale pods to the brink of extinction in the past hundred years. Millions of squid were surviving down there. In the past thirty years, there were specimens of *Architeuthis* living a lifetime without ever being pinged once by a hunting sperm whale. The collective fear of this great cetacean was rapidly dying out as the really old giants continued to go to the bottom for the last time. The new broods didn't know what it was like to fear anything but their own kind.

The incoming sonar pings turned the cool amniotic security of the ocean into an instrument of pain and confusion. The young broods were bleeding chemical messengers of confusion and apprehension into the churning, battering water. The few specimens old enough to know what was about to happen changed colors and began jetting through the writhing community of their brethren, excreting the chemical messengers that filled in the gaps for the youngsters.

The ravenous ones were attacking. The sonar assault continued blanketing the entire squid mass with battering rams of sound waves moving rapidly through the water. And then there was a great roar of cetacean voices riding in the stunning sonar impacts and the chemical memory information was passed from ancient enemy to ancient enemy.

USS Seawolf

THE SOLID LUMINOUS BAND of color on the sonar scope suddenly misted and broke up.

Mr. Markle whooped and made the high-volume report to the control room.

"Conn, sonar! Contact has broken up! They're running, sir!"

"Your enthusiasm is infectious, Mr. Markle," the captain stated. "Continue active pinging. Direct your sonar beams underneath the boat. Keep those bastards down deep while we do this. Tell Mr. Schwarz to report to the diving chamber. The joint task force awaits him."

"Roger, sir!"

Markle clipped the mike back on its stand and began adjusting the sonar beam directional controls. Schwarz still hadn't run for the hatch yet. Markle was a flurry of highly coordinated activity pressing lighted switches and typing commands into the computer.

"Shouldn't you be going to the dive chamber, sir?"

"Just waiting to see what's still underneath us. Remember, I'll be swimming up through the same water those beasts are calling home. I want to know what our separation is going to be."

Markle nodded his understanding. There was no way in hell he would lock out of the sub at this point, with these dangerous creatures in the waters. The screen was painting descending peaks of color as the sonar was reflected back by individual squid targets and the ocean floor.

Then something huge and stationary flashed on the screen and stayed there. It neither fled nor attacked. It was hovering in place, waiting.

Schwarz pointed at the contact.

"That's a big one."

Markle agreed. "No kidding, sir. Half as big as this boat. At least that big, sir."

Schwarz knew that the *Seawolf* was 353 feet in length. That squid down there was at least one-sixty, one-seventy in length.

"How deep is that bastard, Markle?"

"Eight-fifty, sir."

Schwarz did the math. Could that jumbo calamari become a menace to the joint task force in the time it took any of the trained commandos to fin to a surface sixty feet overhead? Not likely. It was a good piece of gambling. The house didn't have the odds on this one.

"Well," Schwarz said on his way out, "if that's as good as it gets, I guess I'll take it."

The Cassiopeia Platform

DAMIEN CASSANDRA stepped off the stairs and exited the core into the lounge. The royal entourage was floating gracefully down to the entry alcove for level six one step at a time. Fairchild had two smoldering women each latched on to an arm. He was making it very clear to Cassandra that the deathtrap springing closed around them was of no consequence to his party. The son of a bitch had immunity. Diplomatic and metaphysical immunity. The UN didn't even offer credentials like that.

The scene in there was like Bedlam acting out 150 different interpretations of the word. The human figurines played the game of Sides on the checkerboard of the bar floor.

It was very tense and would probably escalate into a full-bore shootout between the wise guys and Cassiopeia internal security. None of these men could apparently hold their liquor or their tempers. The two easily identified contingents scrapped and threw taunts into the faces of the others, going as far as firing live rounds into the ceiling to punctuate the seriousness of their words. As any parent would agree, chest thumping and shooting at the ceiling was much better than shooting into each other.

Cassandra was single-minded: find Link Dandridge and kick his ass, then fire him and get some organization going here.

"Dandridge!" he bellowed, his eyes searching the pandemonium for the telltale attire. "I want Link Dandridge front and center, goddammit! And the next guy who sets off another bomb is going over the rail, too!"

The fistfights started breaking up and the two sides

peeled themselves off each other and took a step back, recognizing that, finally, a leader was on hand to take charge.

Cassandra commanded ultimate respect. He was regarded as a wise man, a fair man and a ballsy iron bastard when the times called for such an approach.

The wise guys gave Cassandra the respect of a Don. He was the first outsider ever to be recognized like that by the Mob.

There was one pocket of hostility that couldn't seem to let it go.

Cassandra locked on and headed toward the service doors into the kitchen. Four of the lumberjack-looking Sicilians were pummeling a man with kicks and punches. Some dumb bastard had pushed all the wrong buttons with these guys and was now paying the brutal price. Whoever was getting his butt kicked under this blur of boots and knuckles had enough clout to warrant a five-man security escort. These five guys were disarmed and fighting two of the wise guys each. The wise guys had gotten the better of Cassiopeia's elite and were taking turns restraining and then kicking in the balls each of these black-fatigued Delta wannabes.

Cassandra was going to take back the office of National Security and put somebody in charge who had no affiliation at all with the Central Intelligence Agency. And to hell with the consequences.

"Back off! Back off, goddammit! Who've you got under there?"

The mafiosi backed away from their curb-checked victim.

Cassandra was surprised to see a bloodied, battered Link Dandridge trying to play fetus on the close-cropped carpeting. The CIA agent was beaten almost senseless. Cassandra didn't give a damn. His left foot whistled in and lifted Dandridge's body off the carpet by the rib cage.

"You incompetent idiot! Do you know what explosives in the water might do to the support pylons? We're going to have to send people into each pylon now to inspect every inch of concrete for cracks and leaks! We could still lose this platform to a collapse!"

Dandridge crabbed around on the carpet pathetically, gasping for air and redemption from the nerve-jamming pain. Cassandra felt like he might vomit looking down on this slobbering excuse for a human being. He kicked Dandridge in the ribs again with a cocked right foot.

"Dandridge, you're fired."

He turned on the brass-knuckle enforcers who were working over the Cassiopeia troops.

"Let them go. Whatever this jackass Dandrige did to piss you men off no longer matters. He's out of the loop and I'm taking over his responsibilities. If there's a problem or any heartburn, you come to me and we'll take care of it. Is that cool?"

It was the way he worded things that inspired trust and common bonds.

The mafiosi let the five troopers sag to the floor.

Before he could take charge of the situation, one thundering muzzle-blast echoed across the vast bar floor that made seasoned pistoleros flinch. A tall and very fit man was moving toward them with a huge silver handgun clutched in his left hand, muzzle to the ceiling. Emerging from the kitchen behind him was an attractive strawberry-blond woman followed by a tall man who jerked warily, like some kind of nervous reptile. The cartoonish scarecrow was wielding a can of pepper spray.

The tall soldier's command voice was loud and resonant. He didn't have to shout to be heard.

"I want the ranking man from every East Coast Family to kindly get his ass front and center. Also, whoever is running security for this platform, front and center!"

Cassandra saw recognition in the eyes of this big man as his gaze was drawn to the renegade statesman. This guy was a new player, somebody he'd never seen before.

The president of Cassiopeia was being probed at close range by those unnerving blue eyes.

"Damien Cassandra."

Cassandra nodded. "You have me at a disadvantage, Mr...."

His eyes fell toward the clip-on ID badge the tall man had turned upside down. All that could be seen were the red block letters: PRESS PHOTOG.

"My real name is Pollock. Rance Pollock. Never mind what this says. That's over." Bolan pulled the Devereau cover ID off his vest pocket and tossed it like a shiriken across the lounge.

"I see. Mr. Pollock. And you represent who?"

"I'm an Army liaison to the Justice Department."

"That would be the United States Army and Justice Department."

"Yes."

"I don't take very kindly to United States covert operations being conducted inside my legal sovereign boundaries."

"Regardless of why I'm here, Cassandra, you've got

wounded and noncoms who need to come off this barge. That should be priority one."

Mob leadership was coming forward and joining Bolan and Cassandra.

Cassandra considered what Bolan was saying. "How do you plan on evacuating these people, Mr. Pollock?"

"There is a nuclear attack submarine inbound as we speak."

"I see."

Cassandra looked back in the way he'd come. Fairchild and his two female companions were huddled in what looked like a serious discussion. Cassandra frowned and felt the instant urge to see what had that bunch so suddenly ruffled.

"Excuse me," he said.

Cassandra joined the trio at the center rail overlooking the vast glass dance floor below. Through the sections of the dance floor, the waters below were calming, settling down after a violent stirring. Whatever had been down there was gone now.

He looked across at Fairchild. "I thought I was supposed to see something awesome. Isn't that how you put it?"

Wesson Fairchild's eyes burned with anger as he glared back at Damien Cassandra.

"Show's over, Mr. Cassandra. Do you stay or do you go? No more talk. Please decide. Now."

"I'm evacuating the injured and the women and children."

"That's not good enough. You all must go."

"Well, sir, I guess that if this was a history lesson,

you'd be Santa Ana, I'd be Daniel Boone and this would be the Alamo."

"Precisely what is that supposed to mean?"

Bolan had been monitoring the exchange as he approached from behind. He said, "It means, black priest, that he intends to stand and fight. No surrender."

The dark priest's eyes hardly lingered on Bolan. Fairchild knew a crusader when he saw one.

"Fine. Then you will all become food for the avatar of the dark aeon. Our business is concluded, Mr. Cassandra. There is no need to wish you luck, since you no longer have any. Good day."

13

USS Seawolf

The nuclear submarine glided through the water near the platform at a depth of sixty-five feet. The submarine hovered while the lockout chamber filled with water and equalized. The locks on the big round hatch cover released and the hull lifted away from the dive chamber, allowing the eleven aqua-commandos to fin out in two tight waves and up toward the surface.

The hatch was located just aft of the sail and marked with white painted crosshairs so the Navy's DSRVs—deep-sea rescue vehicles—could identify the hatch easily during an underwater evacuation of the boat. The dive chamber was also the main escape point for the whole submarine. The combat divers kept their eyes focused overhead on the objective and didn't sightsee. Schwarz paused long enough to hook a look down between his fins when he cleared the top of the sail. The water changed color rapidly the deeper down he tried to peer—from coppery green to navy to violet to deep purple to pure darkness. The black hull of the submarine was stark against the lightless abyss straight down.

He knew that somewhere down there where light was filtered out, real monsters were lurking.

The beasts could be in transit right now. On the way back up here. Where the dinner bells were ringing.

That thought made him shudder, and he redirected his eyes toward the surface. He kicked off and dug in, sprinting to recover the lead that the others already had in the time it took him to coast for a look. There was a distant buzzing in the water that was receding. Schwarz thought, small outboard motor while trying not to picture how horrible it would be to become fodder for a giant squid.

The eleven-man strike force divided into two teams and surfaced on each side of the floating section of dock.

The wind and growing whitecaps battered the men's heads with unexpected violence. Schwarz jerked off his face mask and blinked the condensation out of his eyes. He saw the eyes of SEALs Steve Cook and Bobby Gritz in the slapping waters in front of him.

"Hey, guys," he whispered loud enough to be heard. "Your Navy forecasters will have brilliant futures in TV weather. They suck!"

The micro-operations order that had been conducted in the time it took to flood the dive chamber had disseminated that surface weather was calm with misting rain. Only a homicidal psychotic could call these surface conditions calm.

The ravaged dock sections were rocking and rolling in the wild water. It was an exercise in timing for the eleven commandos to jerk themselves, weapons and gear onto the buckling dock.

The special ops troops orientated themselves to the surroundings.

Schwarz was the first one to notice what couldn't

possibly be happening by all the laws of physics and common sense. Through the driving rain and wind, the ocean around the platform seemed to be growing. It was like an encirclement, a 360-degree tidal wave that was piling up higher and higher but something, some force was holding it back.

For the first time in many a moon, Gadgets Schwarz was utterly speechless.

The Cassiopeia Platform

SOMEBODY STANDING on one of the glass deck sections of the dance floor yelled, "Hey, there are men down there! They just came outta the water!"

In the wake of the waterborne attack that the Cassiopeian defenders were still reeling from, the news came as unbelievable. Everyone on both levels of the lounge ran to the center railing or onto the dance floor to get a look. Bolan and Cassandra were already there.

"Those are my reinforcements," Bolan said. "Each one of them is worth a dozen of your triggermen. Do you understand? We can shoot it out or we can do this intelligently. What's your call going to be, Cassandra?"

Cassandra watched the commandos in soaked fatigues and scuba gear make for the stairway up to the deck above, readying weapons as they organized and advanced. Then he looked back at Bolan and studied the icy blue of his eyes.

"You're a man of honor," he stated. "You don't screw over people who don't screw you first, do you?"

"In your own bent way, I feel the same about you. Call it a gut assessment."

"You want to evacuate noncombatants and casualties, is that it?"

"You're in bed with a nest of vipers, Cassandra. You need to turn the page."

"I couldn't have brought all this about without strategic alliances."

"Make new ones."

"Can you protect me from the Central Intelligence Agency? They are the American government. How high does your authority reach, Pollock? Tell me that."

"All the way to the White House."

Cassandra snorted.

"All things end, Cassandra. Take a chance on me."

LINK DANDRIDGE FORCED himself to his knees and breathed away the pain. His fingers probed his ribs and abdomen, feeling for telltale signs of broken bones or a ruptured diaphragm. His damage was mostly cosmetic. One eye almost swollen shut and a gash in his forehead that was bleeding into his good eye. His lips were puffy and cracked, but no teeth had been broken out of the bone.

All he could think about was revenge and turning the tables on that big blue-eyed bastard.

And now he wasn't alone. A SEAL team or some shitload of commandos was coming aboard and they'd probably exfiltrated off a nuclear attack submarine. Dandridge needed some leverage fast.

He stood and looked around. All attention around him was focused on what was going on outside. Nobody was paying him any attention. He looked around on the floor for his Motorola radio. He spotted it and bent with a wince of pain to retrieve it.

"All stations this net. All stations. This is Tiger Shark. Regroup and meet me on level one. Hit the armory and empty it. Bring every weapon we've got and meet me in the factory. How copy, over?"

It was a good copy.

Dandridge smiled, but the pain of it was cleansing, focusing. He moved toward the center core stairwell but decided that the six-level climb was more than he could take right now in his condition. He opted on the elevator instead.

He rode the elevator to the drug processing-environmental engineering control level and locked the car there.

And he waited for his troops to rally there with him.

MALLORY HARMON SKIDDED to a stop and dropped behind the overturned table that Donovan West was using for cover. West was still fumbling with Harmon's Glock. She took it away from him, dropped the magazine and reloaded the stray round that he had ejected. She replaced the magazine and racked the round back into the pipe. Then she handed the weapon back to West.

"I really need to get you on a range, West. This weapons incompetence of yours is dangerous."

"I would welcome the instruction," West said humbly. "Is the safety off?"

"Yeah, it's off. So be careful, okay?"

Another man, dressed like a thermonuclear eruption of garish color, dropped to his knees and hunched down behind the cover of the table. He seemed highly agitated about something. He peeked up over the edge of the makeshift barricade and hooted.

"Oh, Holy Mother! We're in the middle of a goddamn war zone, man! We need to get out of here, fast!"

West looked at the crazed looking individual with obvious distaste.

"Where, pray tell, did you dig up this artifact?"

"Interestingly enough, he saved my ass. So I owe him one."

"What's the score here, FBI? What's the plan?"

Harmon didn't answer immediately. She began ransacking her bag for her tac radio. She pulled out the small device and clipped it to her belt. She donned the headset and turned on the radio.

She tapped the small microphone arm angled in front of her mouth.

"Testing, testing," she said.

A surprised male voice came back with "Identify yourself. Who is this?"

"This is Jezebel, over."

"I don't know you. How'd you gain access to this net?"

Bolan's command voice cut in. "She's part of my insertion team, Ironman. Stand down."

"Roger, Striker."

"Jezebel, what's your twenty?"

"Rallying my resources, over."

"Stand by."

"Standing by."

She checked her surroundings and saw Dandridge beelining it for the stairs, then correcting for the elevator. He was giving hushed instructions into his walkie-talkie. He boarded the elevator and was gone. Then she noticed the Cassiopeia troops and other CIA operatives disengage from the lounge and hit the center core, going up. Her interest and intuition were piqued.

She told her two unlikely backups, "Follow me."

She jogged for the center core and went up to the first

landing, looking up. She waited for West and Garrison to join her. Above her, it looked like the entire Cassiopeian internal security force was hitting the core and running to the top of the platform for something other than a surprise inspection.

She grinned. "The game is afoot."

"What's going on?" West whispered.

"Looks like Dandridge is gonna throw a curveball."

"Yeah, but what are we going to do?"

"We're going to go have a look at what they're up to."

"But they've got a goddamn army up there!" Garrison blurted.

"Hey, you bought the ticket, so take the ride."

THE EXECUTIONER LOWERED the binoculars and handed the glasses to Damien Cassandra. Cassandra adjusted the focus, and the building wall of water leaped into stark resolution through the gray curtain of rain and wind. Gadgets Schwarz, Rosario Blancanales and Carl Lyons stood to the rear, waiting for orders. The SEAL squad was busy moving the ten casualties away from the breached window for triage.

"You don't have to be a psychic to see what's about to happen," Bolan said. "That wall of water is all around us and is almost as high as this platform. I suspect that it'll build up to that point and then come crashing in, swamping Cassiopeia completely and you know what that means, don't you?"

Cassandra lowered the binoculars.

"Then those things will be able to get in here."

"Exactly."

"Jesus Christ. That bastard is the devil."

"Whatever he is, he's holding the ace. We aren't

equipped to deal with whatever it is he's using against us. We've got one option, and we've got to make it happen fast. We have to get the hell off this rock."

Schwarz broke into the discussion.

"Exfil by sub is out. That water wall is gonna be high enough to do the deed before we could even start organizing to get down to the waterline for extraction."

Bolan nodded. "Our only option is to get to the flight deck and take our chances with the helicopters."

"This is pretty heavy weather to try and fly birds out in," Lyons said.

"It's either that or we stay here."

"I designed the environmental sandwich to be water tight," Cassandra told them. "If Cassiopeia does somehow end up underwater, we can hole up on any level above us. Bulkheads will automatically cut off the core if flooding is detected. The ventilation system here is like what they use on submarines. I can't see whatever that bastard is doing as lasting for any length of time. He can't maintain these freak conditions forever."

"Yeah, but we don't know that."

Cassandra thought about it. The big soldier was right.

"Okay, Pollock. Let's try it your way."

Stony Man Farm, Virginia

AARON KURTZMAN WAS tied into the live feed of a surveillance satellite hovering high above the North Atlantic. The sky spy was watching the Cassiopeia platform from an altitude of about twenty-two thousand miles. The mildly inclement weather blanketing the area had literally changed in the wink of an eye.

The change was so sudden and unexpected, it made Kurtzman flinch.

"My God!"

The local conditions of fog and misting rain had transformed into a building hurricane. But it was a hurricane that covered only a dozen square miles. It was a hurricane that didn't seem to move. It was staying in one place—directly on top of Cassiopeia. The infrared scans were telling Kurtzman that the freak storm was building in energy at a geometrical rate, but the storm wasn't moving! For a storm like that to build in strength, the frigging thing had to move.

And then the eye of the storm opened up like a camera iris just south of the platform. The eye of the storm wasn't very big—big enough to comfortably accommodate an aircraft carrier. Kurtzman focused on the storm's eye and had the satellite magnify that region.

There was a vessel in the middle of the eye—a large yacht. The pleasure craft was centered in the sanctuary of the eye, completely safe from the violence of the storm outside that perimeter. The ship wasn't going anywhere. Kurtzman refined the resolution and magnification. Yeah, the yacht's anchor was in the water.

On a hunch, Kurtzman tied into the National Oceanic Atmospheric Administration's climate database, looking for anything else really out of the ordinary. He found it immediately. Freak low tides all along the eastern seaboard. The NOAA's counterparts on the other side of the Atlantic were reporting the same phenomenon. The waterline on both sides of the ocean had receded a hundred yards or more.

Which meant that the sea level out there in the middle of the Atlantic was rising.

Kurtzman made some hasty calculations.

He paled looking at the data.

According to his information, Cassiopeia was underwater now.

He grabbed the red phone and made the panicked call to Hal Brognola.

14

Control Room, USS Seawolf

Commander Len Shaw was keeping an eye on the surface through the optics of the Mk 18 search periscope. He was completing another 180-degree scan when the surface disappeared in a violent wash of foam and bubbles and when the turbulence cleared, all he could see was a greenish haze. The periscope was suddenly underwater. The boat shuddered in the wake of whatever was happening above.

"Captain! I don't know what just happened but we are no longer at periscope depth. The boat either went down or the sea level just rose!"

The helmsman exclaimed, "Sir, the boat hasn't moved, but we're now almost two hundred feet down!"

The green LED readout pegged the sub's depth at 185 feet.

Captain Chance stood from his seat on the raised periscope platform and snatched a mike from overhead. "Sonar, this is the captain. What have you got?"

"Conn, sonar. All clear—wait a minute! They're coming back up! I can't even read the bottom anymore the bastards are so thick! We're about to be hit!"

Chance switched over to the public address mode and sounded the alert.

"All hands—brace for impact! Damage control parties, stand by!"

To the chief of the boat, he yelled, "Cob! Get us the hell out of here! Ahead full!"

"Aye, sir! Ahead full!"

The chief of the boat rattled out headings and speed commands to the planesman and helmsman who signaled the engine room for full speed ahead. The giant submarine lurched forward from a dead stop to max revolutions on the turbine. The control room crew grabbed for handholds to steady themselves.

"Sonar, this is the captain. Are you continuing to transmit the whale calls by hydrophone?"

"No effect, sir! They're not intimidated anymore!"

"How soon until impact?"

"About five seconds, sir!"

"Will we be clear in time?"

"No way, sir!"

"Weapons officer, flood tubes one through four. Prepare to fire on my command."

"Aye, sir! Flooding tubes one through four."

Chance looked at his first officer. They were all about to enter undiscovered country. This was a tactical situation submarine command school had never prepared them for.

And then the squids hit the sub from below.

The Cassiopeia Platform

AND THE WALLS came crashing down.

The lookouts, three mafiosi triggermen from Manhattan, broke away from the windows near the grenade breach and ran like hell for the core.

"There's a tidal wave comin' in!"

Bolan and Cassandra were the stay-behinds while the Mob troops, Able Team and the SEALs went up the stairs in the core en route to the flight deck.

Bolan would never forget the sound of billions of gallons of rioting seawater hitting that man-made structure from all directions at once. The platform rocked and shook and rumbled with the screaming bass notes of total destruction. For a tense few seconds, Bolan thought it was all over right there; the platform was going to be blasted to rubble by all that seawater.

The water swept in through both exits onto the wraparound deck and the window blasted away by the grenade. The three lookouts were swept off their feet and tossed over the center railing into the dance area below, which was already neck deep in water and filling fast. Bolan and Cassandra bounded into the core and up to the second landing. Above them, the stairs were choked with the mafiosi gunners, and the sight of the water flooding in and swirling up around the stairs at the bottom sent those men into a panic. The flooding should have brought the watertight bulkhead down over the opening into the core. But the water kept pouring through.

"Keep it orderly, goddammit!" Bolan yelled over the roar of the water.

The Executioner transmitted, "Pol, what's going on up there? Why the bottleneck?"

Blancanales reported the bad news. "The watertight bulkhead is down up here. We're cut off from the flight deck. Is there another way up there?"

"Wait one."

Bolan turned to Cassandra. "The bulkhead is down on level one. What's up with that?"

The color drained from Cassandra's face as he put two and two together.

"Where's Dandridge?"

THE ONE GROUP on Cassiopeia that could pass for serfs or indentured servants were the chemists and manufacturing technicians. These folk were watched like hawks and worked in three shifts around the clock. They all slept in an open bay barracks on level one, men and women alike. They weren't total slaves; they worked under contract for six-month spells, like deckhands on an Alaskan fishing boat. When they had downtime, they had to ask permission to use the leisure facilities on the levels beneath them. If permission was granted, they had to travel with security escorts or they had to wear a radio telemetry ankle bracelet like convicts under house arrest. The bracelets would deliver a 150,000-volt shock to the wearer if the wearer went anywhere near the marina or the flight deck.

When a labor contract was up, the "chemtech" was paid $30,000 tax-free and wasn't allowed to take another contract for at least three months following. For stress recovery purposes, of course. The techies also signed ominously worded "noncompetition" oaths that would forfeit freedom itself if someone thought they'd take what they'd learned about meth manufacture from Cassiopeia and scale it down for a basement-level operation back in their hometown. The DEA and the IRS were informed of the contract workers' job descriptions upon the completion of a six-month stint in manufacturing, as incentive to stay "honest." If a techie wasn't an American, then their country's counterparts to the DEA and IRS were tattled to and told to keep a close eye on that individual.

Brent Jamison wasn't like the rest of the techs working in manufacturing. He really was under house arrest and his contract was ongoing and nonnegotiable. In the beginning, back when he was originally found and approached, he'd have had a lot better time of it had he knuckled under and not let his ideals get in the way. It wasn't the drug manufacturing that he objected to. Hell, he'd literally written the book on clandestine chemistry. Jamison had written four manuals, which were considered the last word on underground drug manufacturing. To his fans and detractors alike Jamison was known as "Uncle Martin." It was a name lifted from one of the leads of his favorite TV show growing up.

No, it wasn't the drugs that made him resent what he was doing.

It was the organization he was ultimately working for: the Central Intelligence Agency.

Jamison and the rest of his techies had been herded into the barracks and kept under armed guard by two of the "Delta wannabes" when Dandridge exited the elevator, locking it on level one and began barking orders. Dandridge looked like pounded steak. Somebody had just handed the loudmouth bastard his own ass in a brown paper bag, and the sight gave Jamison a modicum of satisfaction. He only wished that whomever had worked over Dandridge like that had finished the job and killed the bastard.

Right now, that was exactly Jamison's goal in life.

Whatever was going on, Jamison knew that it had to be serious.

The two guards were armed with AR-15 assault rifles with backup pistols in quick-draw holsters tied down to their thighs. Jamison's mind was racing through the angles, trying to figure out a way to separate those two and get the weapons. Jamison had numbers on his side: there were thirteen of them. But they were thirteen unarmed egghead types that were scared and that fear would breed hesitation. Not a good mix when planning a jailbreak.

He needed a distraction.

Jamison made eyes with the little brunette he'd been getting fresh with for the past month. Her name was Rebecca, and she was a grad student in organic chemistry at Northwestern University. She took the cue and the two walked to a bunk in the center of the barracks and sat down, backs toward the guards flanking the exit.

"You ever do any theater in high school?" he asked in hushed tones.

"No."

"Well, pretend you did. I'd like you to go into the bathroom and put on a show. Act like you're gonna commit suicide or something. Just make a lot of noise so one or both of those Nazis come running to see what's wrong. I'll do the rest."

"What are you going to do?"

"I want their guns. If we're armed, we're in a much better bargaining position."

"Maybe we should just wait and see what happens."

"Can I rely on you, Beck?"

He could tell that she was fighting to find the courage. He squeezed her shoulder with reassurance.

"Come on. All you've got to do is jump around and act crazy. It's simple."

"You sure?"

He nodded. "It's the only way. Can you do it?"

Finally, she nodded. "Okay."

She got up and went into the bathroom, and Jamison

moved back in that direction as well, waiting for her to
start the show.

BOLAN INSTRUCTED Blancanales over the tac radio to
drop down to the second level and get everyone out of the
core while he and Cassandra bulled their way up through
the crowd. The air pressure inside the core was keeping
the water from rising any higher than level six. But the
air in there was starting to stink of ammonia, and the waters were churning down there as tentacles and whip arms
were lashing out like feelers, probing for something to eat.
Bolan knew that the really big ones weren't going to get
into the platform but the smaller ones, the ten, twenty and
thirty footers would have no problem swimming into the
structure to hunt for prey. As long as the water didn't rise
any higher and nothing else was breached, they might
have a fighting chance at survival.

Bolan knew that the drug-processing level had none
of the huge glass ports that every other level was ringed
with. For safety and fire reasons alone, the level was
self-contained and hermetically sealed off from the rest
of the structure. They had to find a way up there or they
were all going to die.

The Executioner had no doubts about that.

Bolan yelled up the concrete shaft, "Keep it moving! We're vulnerable in here! Get the hell out on level
two! Move! Move!"

Bolan and Cassandra reached the alcove opening
onto level three and he heard the sobbing and hysteri-
cal voices of the women out on the mezzanine.

The dancers and hookers. He'd forgotten all about
them.

"Keep this mob moving up to level two," Bolan told

Cassandra. "I'm going to police up these women and I'll join you there."

Cassandra nodded. He said, "Good luck."

Bolan bounded out onto the mezzanine and shouted, "Listen up! You all need to follow me up the stairs as high as we can go! You are all in grave danger if you stay here!"

The women were dragging bags full of their belongings.

Bolan yelled, "Leave the personal stuff! We don't have time for it! Get in this stairwell now!"

The women did as they were told and ran past Bolan into the core. "Go up!" he ordered as they filed by. A straggler came running out of one of the branching hallways in a panic.

She stopped as if paralyzed, with both hands pressed against her ears.

"Someone, help me please," she cried.

Bolan yelled at her over the roar of rampaging water. "Get up the stairs! Go! Go!"

Something in his tone broke through her terror, and she ducked into the alcove and up the stairs. He cleared the alcove right behind her and jogged to the right, pounding up the stairs as the water blew through and pummeled the reinforced concrete of the core on the other side. Bolan caught a glimpse of something huge and purple rocketing over the railing in all that water and splatter against the concrete wall. It dropped down the shaft with the torrent fall of ocean. With any luck, the thing was dead.

The stakes just got worse.

With this breach, the entire platform was going to flood below level two. Level two was ringed with the same glass windows that everything below level one had. And level one was locked off to them.

Bolan knew that those things would learn by example. When one made the breach, they'd all know how to get in.

The doomsday numbers were falling against them.

It would take a miracle to save them now.

USS Seawolf

THE SQUID SHOT UP around the huge nuclear submarine like bullets and ricocheted off the hull. Each strike, multiple hits at a time, rocked the sub.

Captain Chance shouted over the emergency Klaxons, "Helm! Maintain speed and course! Get us the hell out of here!"

And then it was over. The ride smoothed out and they were clear of the field of squid.

The captain snatched the mike from overhead.

"Damage control parties report back to control! Assess damage!"

Damage control teams began reporting back. Minor leaks and interruptions in electrical power were the worst of it. This new class of submarine was earning her keep. She was the best of the best.

"Conn, sonar! Sir, you need to check this out!"

Chance keyed the mike. "I'm on my way."

He returned the mike to its stand.

"XO, you have the conn. I'll be in sonar."

"Aye, sir."

The captain stepped into the cramped sonar shack and stood behind Mr. Markle.

"What have you got, Mr. Markle?"

Markle removed his headset and handed it to the captain.

"Listen to that, sir."

Chance frowned but didn't say anything. He put the headset on and his eyes widened.

"What the hell is that?"

It was the eeriest thing he'd ever heard. From down in the depths came a chattering clatter, like bones being pounded together. It almost sounded like Morse code. And then from above, in answer, were dozens of the same kind of bone-on-bone taps. It was like an order being given and then a battalion of subordinates was repeating the order, telegraphing it through the ranks.

Unbelievable.

Chance scanned the sonar screen. There was one gigantic contact beneath the submarine, and that was the source of the original clatter that the monsters above were answering to.

The leader of the pack was identified.

Like a good sniper, Chance knew what had to be done. He snatched the mike off the console and keyed it.

"Cob, this is the captain. Make your depth eight-five-zero. Fifteen degrees down bubble, ahead full. When the ship reaches depth bring us about hard to a heading of one-five-six and hover. Weapons officer, stand by to fire tubes one through four on my command. XO, I will be commanding the boat from sonar."

The commands were echoed from the control room and the sub made a high-speed dive into the darkness, coming around to bring all tubes to bear.

It was a showdown between Nature's most fearsome and man's technological best. The battle of the leviathans was on.

The Cassiopeia Platform

LEVEL TWO WAS the hydroponics bay. Row after row of shelf gardens stacked eight high, growing some of the best marijuana this side of Amsterdam. From all around, the place sounded like pure hell. It was that pounding on the glass from outside.

Bolan needed options, fast.

Schwarz laid it all out for the Executioner.

"To blast through that steel bulkhead, we're going to need more than we've got. However, the ceiling is reinforced concrete. A ring charge should punch us through with no problem."

Bolan knew what was overhead. He'd already had the walk-through.

"We just can't arbitrarily punch a hole in the ceiling. They've got a major industrial meth operation going overhead. If you put your charges under one of those chemical vats, this whole place is going to the moon. We have to have precise placement knowledge."

"We're going to have to take a chance, Striker. We don't have any other choice."

Bolan looked around him. All those faces looking to him for salvation. He scanned the crowd for her face. But she wasn't there. His eyes narrowed.

"Jezebel, this is Striker. What's your twenty, over?"

SHE PEERED over the fifty-five-gallon drums of toluene and watched the opposition. In her earpiece, the colonel was calling her station.

"Striker, this is Jezebel, over," she whispered. "We are in the lab where they make all the drugs. What's going on at your end?"

"We need that watertight bulkhead raised. At the very least, you need to guide us to a clear area on your floor where a ring charge isn't going to set off every chemical vat up there. Can you find something to pound on the floor with?"

She had the butt of her weapon. She immediately got her bearings. Behind her position was open floor. She ran, staying low while motioning with her hands for Garrison and West to hold in place.

She started giving instructions.

She consulted the small compass on the wristband of her watch.

"Move out on a forty-seven from the core. I'd estimate it to be about twenty yards. Get near there and listen for my rapping from above. Place the charge there."

"We're moving."

Harmon started hammering on the concrete floor with the butt of the H&K .45 SpecOps pistol.

At that same moment, from the other side of the huge room, somebody was yelling, "Hey, we got a medical emergency in here! Hey, we need help!"

She looked up briefly to see security troops running toward double doors in the wall on that end. The troops disappeared inside and then the shooting began.

She hammered the concrete harder.

GADGETS SCHWARZ climbed the steel shelves and ripped the drop ceiling away. With a sweep of his arm he cleared the shelf of foot-tall marijuana plants growing out of rock wool cubes and threw the demolitions kit onto the open shelf. He quickly adhered the ring charge to the concrete ceiling and primed it with electric blasting caps. He dropped back to the floor, unraveling wire from the fire device as he went. He didn't bother testing the circuit. It was do or die.

"I'm ready!" he yelled. "Fire in the hole!"

Bolan raised a clenched fist. It was infantry sign language for "freeze!"

"Mallory, get clear!" he transmitted. "Take cover! You have about three seconds!"

USS Seawolf

MARKLE REPORTED. "We have more range than we need to lock and arm, sir. Twenty-one hundred meters from the target."

Over the intercom, Cob reported, "Heading one-five-six, sir. We are hovering."

The captain keyed the mike.

"Weapons officer, fire tubes one through four!"

"Firing one through four! Aye, sir!"

The big submarine shuddered as the four fish left the tubes and accelerated to an intercept speed of about sixty knots.

"We are locked on the target!" Markle exclaimed.

Chance watched the sonar readout as the four fish blipped across the screen, narrowing the gap.

And just when the fish were ready to do their ugly work, the target did the unexpected.

And suddenly the hunter became the hunted.

IT BECAME aware of a disturbance in the surrounding water. Four fish-things that weren't fish, which weren't alive, were vectoring in rapidly. The four fish-metal-things had been expelled from the giant whale-thing that wasn't a whale.

The avatar reoriented itself in the water, pointing its

gigantic torpedo-shaped body in the direction of the intruder. It waited.

Its timing was supernatural. At the last possible second, it sucked a huge volume of water into its mantle and vented it through the fleshy funnel on the side of its head. The avatar dived under the incoming torpedoes and came back up, charging down the enemy submarine with the speed of a missile in the water. The giant squid was a natural water-jet engine, and this monster could maintain a fifty-knot speed easily.

The Mk 48 ADCAP torpedoes turned wildly in the water, active sonar pinging to reestablish the target lock.

Two of the fish lost the target and careened off into the hazy near-black murk. The remaining fish reestablished the target lock and changed course to follow the charging monster that was on a collision course with the Navy's finest nuclear attack submarine.

That monster squid was going to catch the sub and then the torpedoes were going to catch the squid.

A $2 billion submarine was about to go to the bottom in a rain of twisted metal and squid chunks.

The Cassiopeia Platform

DAMIEN CASSANDRA had given Bolan the layout of the processing bay and told him where environmental engineering was located up there. The master panel controlling the emergency bulkheads was located in that area, and that was Bolan's objective once the breach was made.

Bolan put Cassandra in charge of the stay-behinds until a foothold above could be taken.

He told the Cassiopeia boss, "Once we've got fire superiority, the women come up the hole first. If I see any hard cases trying to get up in front of a woman, I'll shoot them myself. Understood?"

"If some punk tries that, I'll shoot them first. And, Pollock, watch where the hell you're shooting. Everything up there can explode if sparks start flying and for God's sake—no grenades."

"That's why we're going in first and these wise guys are staying down here on standby."

The hydroponics level was almost as big as the one above and the big glass picture windows that were supposed to be almost apocalypse-proof were twelve feet wide and ceiling high. Between every window was a ten-foot section of solid concrete. It was like that all the way around the perimeter and when the platform wasn't underwater, it afforded breathtaking views in all directions.

Every one of those glass slabs was under attack from outside. The sound of those hundreds of chitinous beaks jackhammering against the glass was unnerving to say the least. Bolan knew that the monsters would ultimately crash through. It was only a matter of time and force versus resistance.

The water level in the core was as high as the landing inside the alcove. Tentacles were tentatively slithering out of the water, feeling for anything that reacted like prey. A crew of triggermen was keeping an eye on the creatures, armed with baseball grenades for when the time came. Once the bulkhead above was raised, they were going to start dropping the bombs into the water, letting the lethal eggs blow underwater and send the refugees up ten or fifteen at a time between the blasts.

It was a good plan.

All they needed was the time to make it work.

Bolan, Able Team and the SEALs hunkered down to the left and right under the ring charge on the ceiling and braced themselves. The hole was going to be big enough to allow two large men to pass through at a time.

Bolan nodded to Schwarz. "Blow it."

The electronics expert yelled, "Fire in the hole!" and hit the button.

The concrete overhead blew in a big oval of flash and noise. The concrete disintegrated into dust and pebble-sized chunks, and the blast was directed upward and out.

Bolan didn't wait for the air to clear. He was up and scaling the shelves. Carl Lyons was right beside him. Both of them vaulted through the breach and ran low for the line of barrels where Harmon, West and Garrison had taken cover. Lyons had the SWA-12 auto shotgun slung across his back and his right fist was filled with his Colt Python .357 Magnum pistol.

Behind them, Blancanales and Schwarz emerged from the breach and then the SEALs.

Bolan went to ground next to Mallory Harmon.

"What have we got?"

"Maybe twenty internal security goons, Dandridge and a couple of his fellow field agents. I think the drug techs are launching a coup. They yelled for help and lured a group of the goons in, there was some shooting and now it's a standoff."

Bolan peered over the top of the drum in front of him. A fire team of security guards was moving toward the barrels, investigating what the sharp explosion was all about. Bolan fired one thundering round over their heads.

"Drop your weapons and surrender now!"

The five security men found themselves staring into twelve serious looking muzzles. They knew a losing bet when they saw one. All five dropped their assault rifles and reached for the sky.

The remaining security troops were behind cover, their weapons trained on the workers' barracks. They lifted and shifted to cover the new arrivals.

"You've got two seconds to lower your weapons or we'll put you down!" Bolan yelled at them.

The staging area for the barrels of toluene was located adjacent to the huge vat that electrically oxidized the toluene. Jake Lassiter edged around from the rear, following the curvature of the vat and put two rounds into the right side of Commander Luke Flynn as he was pivoting to engage the peripheral threat.

The SEAL CO was kicked in the ribs by the bullet strikes and swatted against the drums. The three other SEALs with Flynn on the right flank swung around and rattled bursts from their 9 mm MP-5 SD-5 subguns. The rounds were subsonic loads that greatly increased the effectiveness of the weapon system's built-in suppressor. The bullets chattered like tearing cloth, and the muzzle-blast was negligible.

The dozen hits unzipped Lassiter's guts.

The security guards assumed Lassiter's first shot was aimed in their direction and opened fire themselves. Bolan triggered the Desert Eagle. One thundering round blew the middle shooter's chest apart like ripe summer squash. The guys who had given up dropped to the deck and rearmed themselves. These five guys crawled in five different directions to take cover. SEAL Fire Team 2 took out two more behind cover and forced the rest to keep their heads down.

Bolan saw Link Dandridge bolt out from behind a hydrogenation vat and run as best as he could for a victim of multiple curb-checks. Dandridge was going for the louvered metal door marked overhead in big stenciled red letters: ENVIRONMENTAL ENGINEERING. The big metal door was rolled up.

"Check fire!" Bolan yelled. "I'm going in!"

He ran out from behind the barrels and took off across the vast concrete bay.

Dandridge was going for the bulkhead controls, and the Executioner had to stop him before he could destroy the control circuitry.

He heard the muffled screams wafting up suddenly out of the breach, and washing over the shrieks of the women was the unmistakable din of flooding waters shooting into the hydroponics bay under high pressure.

There was no more time left on the clock.

The bulkhead had to come up.

MALLORY HARMON decided to help the people on the lower level. She dropped through the big oval hole in the floor and landed on top of the shelving directly below. There was about four and a half feet of clearance between the top of the shelf and the concrete ceiling. Her head and shoulders were poking up through the hole. She jumped to the deck and announced authoritatively, "Okay, people, let's go! You, ma'am, with the little boy, let's go. You two are priority."

Harmon pushed the woman in front of the shelf.

She pried the little boy out of his mother's arms and placed him on her back.

The woman didn't have to be persuaded. She climbed the shelving and hoisted herself through the hole. The rest of the women went up three at a time and the water was swirling waist deep around Harmon.

One squid had made it through one of the gigantic panes of glass on the opposite side of the bay. The ocean rushed into the huge room through the twelve-by-four-teen hole, and the killer squid were sucked in so thick that the jam-packed opening actually blocked the water until one or two could slither out. The water blew through the Medusa clog and scattered the seventy-odd squid almost to the core.

The bigger specimens were propelled into the bay like missiles and crashed through the tall shelving.

The street soldiers were in a frenzy. The ten- and twenty-footers were into their ranks quickly, since these versions could dart right between shelving. The bigger squid had to swim through the boiling canals flowing around shelving units to get to their prey. The guys with grenades were yanking pins and throwing the bombs as fast as they could. Shotguns and Uzis boomed and rat-tled. The screaming of men being hit three at once and torn apart was horrific.

Harmon scrambled up the shelving and was spring-ing up on top when the unit she was on buckled and col-lapsed beneath her feet. Her fingers latched on to the lip of concrete, and she was dangling from the hole in the ceiling. She did a chin-up and poked her head through the hole.

"West! Garrison! Give me a hand."

The operative and journalist spun, and West reacted first. He dropped the pistol and bolted away from cover in a flat-out run. Garrison followed. West skidded to a stop and dropped to his knees, grabbing her under the armpits. He started to pull her up. The water exploded beneath her, and tentacles constricted around her waist and left thigh.

"Help me, Garrison! For God's sake, man! The beast has got her!"

But Harmon didn't scream; she gritted her teeth and fought with all her strength to hold on to West and the concrete edge.

Garrison loped up off to one side and yelled, "I'll spray the bastard!"

He sprayed an ineffectual cloud of pepper spray into the hole and West bellowed, "Help me hold on to her, you lunatic!"

Garrison pivoted to grab the FBI agent by the shoulders of her vest. The beast's whip arm shot out of the hole and slammed West away like a gnat. West hit Garrison, who fell headfirst into the hole, going in over the top of Harmon. His lanky legs smacked her face and jaw and in the wash of pain, she lost her grip.

Harmon was jerked backward and into the water.

DANDRIDGE'S AIM was shaky with pain. Blood in his eyes wasn't helping him with the task.

He raised the .45 ACP Colt Government pistol to start popping off rounds into the emergency bulkhead control panel. But his left leg was blown in two while the world exploded with fury and noise. Dandridge screamed, almost blacking out. He was pitched to the floor and the pistol was no longer in his hand. His grip on the world was getting dark.

Bolan didn't waste any time on growling tough-guy

eulogies to his fallen enemy. He ran to the panel and punched the override button that raised the bulkhead.

"The bulkhead is up!" he yelled over the command net. "Get those men out of there!"

The firefight was already over. The security team had been beaten like gongs in about a minute of tense exchanges.

The Executioner could do nothing to help Dandridge.

USS Seawolf

CAPTAIN CHANCE braced himself against the bulkhead as he ordered the boat into an emergency dive.

"Cob, go deep!" he yelled into the keyed mike. "We have to beat those torpedoes to their implosion depth or we're all dead!"

The deck sloped sharply as Cob pointed the bow into a twenty-degree down bubble.

"Engine room, ahead full!"

His eyes were locked on to the sonar readout. He was reading the target blips and the ranges that were diminishing too rapidly. The squid was almost on top of them. The beast would just be getting a good grip on the hull of the giant submarine when those two fish would catch up to the target.

He needed something to slow that bastard. Just a heartbeat or two of extra run-time was all he was looking for.

And he had an idea.

"Torpedo room! Load a dummy fish and fire! Don't wait for the command to be echoed! Load and shoot!"

"Tube one flooding and firing!" the weapons officer reported. "Snap shot away!"

The sub shuddered slightly as the fish shot out the

tube amidships and raced in front of the diving leviathan. The fish hooked a U-turn and active sonar immediately acquired the target. The fish accelerated to attack speed and raced on a collision course toward the charging sea monster.

The avatar diverted slightly and attacked its attacker. The sleek training torpedo flew through the thrashing tentacles and impaled the squid right between its huge eyes, just under the mantle. The squid reversed course, trying to recoil from the fish stuck in its brain, and the *Seawolf* opened up a small gap before the two torpedoes detonated on each side of the crazed squid, erasing the monster from the depths.

The shock front hit the submarine aft and almost flipped the boat propeller over bow. When the sub drivers had the boat leveled back out in the wake of the shock front, Chance gave the order to surface.

"XO, get us on the roof! Emergency blow!"

IT WAS AS IF a bubble had burst and the spell was broken.

The laws of physics and nature went back to normal. The sea level dropped back to where it should have stayed all along, and the water levels inside the platform reversed. Some of the squid were washed back out into the ocean below as the water succumbed to gravity. Most of the giant cephalopods were trapped and beached inside the environmental sandwich and when caught out of water, the monsters were sitting ducks.

"Somebody get a gun over here!" Donovan West screamed. "Dr. Harmon is going to be killed!"

Suddenly, a huge blond man stood over the hole with

an auto shotgun blasting at the monster below. Harmon was fighting to get her weapon out as the tentacles were pulling her into the snapping beak.

Lyons jumped through the hole and planted his boot heels into the slimy flesh of the twenty-five-footer and emptied the 12-gauge mix of slugs and steel BBs into its upturned eye.

Harlan Garrison had a twisted piece of steel tubing in hand and was thrashing on a micro-*Architeuthis* wrapped around his thigh, a tiny beak coring a thimble-sized chunk of meat out of his leg.

"Jesus! It's biting my fucking leg off!"

Lyons leaped off the body of the monster and threw Garrison to the flooded deck, only inches deep now. He stomped on the squid's head and let the shotgun dangle on its lanyard. He drew a Ka-bar knife from his assault vest and cut the tail off the four-foot-long squid, killing it instantly.

The mafiosi soldiers were having a turkey shoot now.

15

The Bermuda Conservatory

The yacht looked like a big knife in the water, a giant silver blade designed to cut through the ocean with great efficiency and very little resistance. The sharp lines of the hull were absolutely stark and menacing in the dawn's early light. The ship was anchored in the middle of the private cove bordered on one side by a white cliff face that rose about sixty feet above the transparent blue waters. The sundeck on the yacht was almost flush with the top of the cliffs. The silver aluminum hull and superstructure was stacked four decks high and almost two hundred feet in length; this yacht was the ultimate private pleasure craft.

The raiding party entered the cove by sea after making a submarine lockout from the submerged USS *Seawolf* hovering in shallow water at periscope depth less than two miles off the northern coast of Bermuda. The war party paddled stealthily into the cove in two Combat Rubber Raiding Craft—CRRC—which was a fancy Navy appellation for the standard black Zodiac inflatable boat favored by all branches of service within the special operations community. CRRC number one ferried SEAL Fire Team 2, Bolan and Special Agent Mallory Harmon. CRRC number two was manned by SEAL Fire Team 1. The personnel in both of the boats stayed low to avoid needlessly silhouetting against the horizon.

The Executioner was lying prone at the bow, watching the twelve o'clock through the twenty-power scope of the Haskins .50-caliber sniper rifle. His finger was lightly curled around the trigger, and his thumb was resting on the select fire switch. In a heartbeat, he could have the safety off and be engaging targets downrange up to a mile and a half away. The Haskins was a bolt-action single-shot sniper rifle that weighed almost twenty pounds with bipod and scope attached. The weapon was standard SEAL issue.

To Bolan's left and right were two SEAL gunners. The man on the left was looking over the sights of an M-16/M-203 combo and covering the nine to eleven o'clock positions. Right flank was watching one to three o'clock through the iron sights of an M-60 machine gun. He had an MP-5 with attached suppressor slung across his back for use once the yacht was boarded. Harmon was crouched in the middle of the CRRC directly behind Bolan. The SEAL commo man was aft in the coxswain's position, operating the outboard engine, a superquiet fifty-five horsepower motor with an eighteen gallon fuel bladder, which gave the little black Zodiac a range of about sixty-five miles and a top speed of twenty knots.

The two CRRCs stayed abreast of each other with a separation of about thirty yards. The raid party entered the cove without fanfare and approached the silent yacht from the rear.

The Executioner was scanning the pleasure craft

from waterline to radar masts through the scope. He didn't see any movement or any clues that the ship was even inhabited. She sat there, anchored in glass smooth waters, deathly still like a ghost ship.

The entire raiding party was equipped with PRC-126 tactical radios with VOX throat mikes. The radio traffic was being kept to an absolute minimum. *Seawolf* had her antenna mast up and was monitoring the team's traffic, retransmitting every piece of traffic received back to the Pentagon via satellite.

"There's a large opening aft of the target on the waterline," Bolan transmitted. "It looks like a garage of some kind. I see several Jet Skis. Suggest we board the target there."

There was a burst of static, then Lieutenant Commander James Starbuck, now the acting CO, replied, "Roger. I agree. Let's board this bitch right in her ass."

The coxswains of both CRRCs adjusted their courses and made for the open garage bay at the waterline. The SEAL commander designated Bolan's boat to be the first one in while CRRC number two held back in overwatch.

The coxswain laid on a burst of speed to quickly cover the last fifty yards to the target. A small platform sat at water level for loading and unloading Jet Skis or swimmers and the Zodiac powered right out of the water and slid into the garage interior on momentum without a hitch. Bolan abandoned the sniper rifle and was first on deck. He yanked the huge silver Desert Eagle autoloader from side leather and went down on one knee while covering the single hatch ahead while the SEALs and Harmon unassed the CRRC.

The only sounds came from the gentle lap of the water around the loading platform, the creak of the hull as the huge yacht swayed slightly in the cove on the anchor line and the muffled metallic scraps of small arms on vest webbing.

"All clear," Bolan sent.

"Roger."

The second Zodiac rushed in moments later. Their coxswain cut the engine from ten yards out and coasted into the garage with more stealth. The SEAL CO assigned the coxswain and the twelve o'clock man to stay with the boats and secure the rear. The CO moved forward with his remaining soldier and joined Bolan. He grinned at the Executioner through his green face.

"You look like a guy who wants to take point."

"That's where the action is," Bolan stated.

The CO pivoted on his knee and pointed at his 203 gunner.

"Sensor sweep," he said softly, pointing to the bulkhead in front of them. The 203 gunner nodded and pulled out a small pistol grip device that looked like a stun gun. The SEAL went to the bulkhead and moved along the wall. The device was an extremely sophisticated heartbeat sensor capable of tracking human heartbeats through thick concrete. The device worked by detecting the unique ultra-low frequency electrical field given off by a beating heart. The Navy man completed his sweep and gave a thumbs-up.

"No readings," he whispered.

Bolan didn't have to be told what to do. He moved into position in front of the closed hatch. The 203 gunner took the right side and the 60 gunner, packing the MP-5 now, flattened against the wall to the left of the hatch. Bolan popped the hatch and bounded into the engine room. The two Caterpillar marine engines with dual turbochargers and fuel injection dominated the room. The engines were equipped with vibration dampers, and the walls were constructed with soundproof paneling.

Bolan went straight in about fifteen feet and went down on one knee, covering everything to the front with his Desert Eagle. His flankers went through the hatch one by one. The SEAL commander and Harmon followed and crouched behind Bolan. The two trailing SEALs moved out front and took up new positions to the right and left of the next hatch, the next danger area. The sensor man went forward next and did another sweep.

Thumbs-up. "No readings."

Bolan stood and shoved the hatch open, bulling through into a narrow corridor. Rich nautical blue carpeting compressed under his dive boots, and the walls were paneled in dark walnut. Two doorways lined each side of the hallway, all of them closed. The four SEALs crept through the hatch into the corridor and split into two teams, taking the first cabin to the right and left. The search teams went into the cabins and reappeared quickly.

Both teams reported "Clear," and moved forward to take the next two doors in line. Bolan waited at the end of the corridor, in front of another closed hatch and held in place for the two teams to clear this sector before continuing forward. The SEAL commander and Harmon came in behind the two clearing teams. As soon as the first two cabins were cleared, Harmon checked out the rooms herself. When she emerged again, the SEALs and Bolan were waiting for her.

"Did we overlook something, Special Agent Harmon?" the SEAL commander asked.

"No," Harmon snapped. "I'm looking for things that you aren't."

"I hope you're not holding out on us, Special Agent. If one of my men—"

Bolan intervened. "Commander Starbuck, Agent Harmon is with my team and she's acting on orders from my end. No unnecessary bullshit, okay?"

The SEAL commander shrugged. "Roger that, Colonel."

"Go ahead, Agent Harmon. Check them out. We'll wait."

She ducked into the second cabin on the left, rooted around quickly, crossed into the corridor again and went into the second cabin on the right. She spent a few seconds checking drawers, bookshelves and the head, and rejoined the assault force.

Her report was a simple. "Nada."

The sensor sweep was another bust. With the nod from the sensor man, Bolan opened the hatch and moved through quickly. The corridor on the other side was shorter and narrower. There were no more doors to the right or left, just one directly to the front. Bolan got there, leaned against the door and listened. He opened the door without waiting for the sensor man to give him a green light. He knew there was nobody on the other side. In fact, his guts were telling him very clearly that the whole yacht was going to be like this first deck—empty and abandoned.

The Executioner stepped into a cramped alcove. A tight spiral companionway to the main deck was directly in front of him, a closed door to his left, an open one to the right. Bolan went to the right and stepped into the crew's lounge. There were some light entertainment magazines on a coffee table, some books and popular videos on the shelves. Everything was very neat and orderly.

Bolan went back to the doorway and poked his head through. Two SEALs were checking the room behind the closed door. It was the ship's laundry. The SEAL commander left a man to cover the stairs. He quickly explained the rules of engagement.

"If anyone tries to come down and they're armed, take them out. If they're unarmed, take them into custody. You know the drill."

Harmon didn't wait for the clearing teams. She insinuated herself around Bolan and through the doorway into the crew lounge. She quickly inspected the area and continued forward. Bolan whirled after her and hooked the hood of her wet suit, yanking her back into the lounge.

"Not so fast. We do this by the book. You get too eager, you make mistakes. That's when you're going to get killed."

"Or get one of us killed," the SEAL commander added. "We should have left you on the submarine."

She looked at the SEAL commander with anger in her eyes, then returned her gaze to Bolan.

"Sorry, Colonel. You're right."

Forward of the crew's lounge were the crew cabins—six postage-stamp-sized cubbyholes. Bolan continued forward. The corridor terminated at another companionway leading to the main deck. To the right and left were small entry alcoves that opened into two larger rooms that might have started out at the factory as "crew cabins" but had been extensively redecorated and furnished since leaving the shipyard.

The Executioner whistled. "Bingo."

Harmon was right on his heels as he took the room

to the port and examined the dungeon and its trappings. Harmon's mind was instantly adding up the uses and purpose each item in there served.

"You seen anything like this before?" she asked.

Bolan replied through gritted teeth, "Yeah. Unfortunately I have."

"Do you have any idea what these two rooms are used for?"

"I have an idea."

"Specifically, trauma induction to facilitate the splintering and compartmentalization of personality."

Bolan had seen many a torture room over the miles and the years. While this room wasn't being used to create turkeys, the end result was very similar: another human being with a shredded soul and an erased personality. These bastards used heinous violation and high tech hypno-trances to rend and tear the psyche, leaving wounds that left no scars.

The walls were bare metal, as were the floor and ceiling. There wasn't a bunk or toilet. On the bow facing wall, a set of chains and manacles for the wrists and ankles of the victim were welded to square iron plates bolted into the bulkhead. A bank of halogen lights was mounted to the ceiling in a strip, and the reflectors were aimed at the chains on the wall. A small steel table, bolted to the deck, was located below and to the rear of the bank of lights. A programming console controlled a stereo sound system and the lights above. Next to the console was a device that was obviously used to deliver electric shocks to the manacled victim. The voltage could be increased or decreased with the twist of a dial. Several strands of thin cable were coiled and neatly banded, one end hooked into the machine. Three Panther stun guns were lined up on the table as well, one designed to deliver 100,000 volts, the middle 200,000 and the last packed a 300,000-volt punch. On the wall opposite the manacles were various sex toys and S/M equipment hanging from neatly machined quarter-inch steel pegs. And in the corner, trained at an angle toward the chains on the wall, was the digital video camera. No rape dungeon was complete without that.

On the other side of the corridor, the four SEALs were gaping at the starboard dungeon's equipment. Bolan and Harmon stepped back into the cramped corridor. The SEAL commander looked agitated.

He stepped out of the dungeon and leaned in close to Bolan.

"Just what kind of sado-pornographic studio is that in there?"

"That's highly classified, Commander," Bolan replied. "Rest assured that we've seen this kind of thing before."

"Really? What does your sidekick there do again?"

"I'm from the FBI, Commander Starbuck," Harmon snapped. "I'm assigned to the Behavioral Sciences Unit. We hunt serial killers and sexual predators."

"So we're going after Hannibal Lecter and not Dr. No. Is that your expert opinion here?"

Harmon's eyes flared. "Sir, have you always been a penis with ears or is this something new for you?"

The look on the SEAL commander's face in the wake of that query was nothing less than remarkable. Bolan knew that SEALs could be some of the most swaggering bunch of arrogant cowboys this side of the French foreign legion. But he'd never seen one knocked speechless in one sentence by a petite but feisty FBI agent.

"What we're both driving at, Commander," Bolan said,

"is that we're probably not going to be finding any Buck Rogers weather weapons on board this yacht or on shore."

Bolan could see that the SEAL commander was smarting hard over Harmon's remark and the wheels in his brain were spinning out trying to find a comeback with as much barb. He barely heard what Bolan had said.

Finally, the SEAL commander broke the stare down and said, "Snappy little...tamale, isn't she?"

The claustrophobic stairwell opened up on the bow with no access to the main deck. The clearing team led by Bolan reversed course and went back down to the lower deck. The SEAL commander had radioed his guard on the spiral stairs to move up to the main deck and hold in place until the clearing team linked up with him. The dead end changed that plan. The SEAL commander was taking a breath to update his man on the main deck that they were going to be coming up the spiral instead. The stair guard stepped on the CO, beating the SEAL commander to the transmission.

"One, this is five. I have a body up here."

"Five, One. Roger. Hold in place. Be advised we are moving back the way we came and will link up with you via the spiral stairs. How copy?"

"Roger. Good copy."

A body. Bolan made his way back through the crew cabins and into the alcove with the spiral stairs. He didn't bother with being tactically correct. He pounded up the stairs with the Desert Eagle at the ready and into another small alcove. There were two doors to the right and left. The left door was ajar and that's where Bolan went. Harmon was right behind him. They found themselves in a spacious corridor that jogged to the right almost immediately and passed a horseshoe-shaped set of

stairs that climbed to the bridge deck. Bolan stayed
dead on course and straight-armed through double doors
into the main dining room.

The contrast between the cramped crew areas and the
palatial layout for the jet-setters was like a neat little lesson in social stratification.

The room encompassed the actual dining area and to
the rear, a huge recreation area equipped with posh
sofas, top of the line entertainment systems, a pool table
and a big-screen TV. The dining table was an oak mon-
strosity that dominated the center of the dining area and
elevated two steps up from the deck. The table and elevated platform it was bolted onto was shaped like a
stretched octagon and had fourteen place settings for
VIPs. The floor was decadently carpeted in the exact
shade of Federal Reserve green, and the walls were paneled with real oiled mahogany.

The spread-eagled and disemboweled man adorn-
ing the oak table ruthlessly clashed with the entire
decor. It wasn't quite like putting a vase of roses in the
center of the table to add a little color and beauty. And
the smell in there wouldn't be bringing anyone running for dinner.

The four SEALs burst into the luxurious dining room
behind Bolan and Harmon. They all stepped up the two
stairs and positioned themselves around the table in a half
horseshoe, looking down at the corpse without comment.

"I guess we *are* looking for Hannibal Lecter," the
SEAL commander muttered.

Harmon shook her head and chuckled. She stepped
closer to the table and leaned over the body. At the same
time, something crunched under her dive boots. She
straightened and looked down at the floor. There was a

broken piece of dowel, very thin, almost like a match-
stick. She crouched and picked up the two sections,
frowning. Then she spotted another of the thin wood
sticks on the carpet and then another and another. The
SEALs were still checking out the body, but Bolan was
watching her. He could tell she was on to something.

Harmon went around the table, looking down at the
money-green carpet, spotting the little reeds and picking them up. By the time she had circled the table once,
she had a handful of the matchsticklike dowels. By then
all eyes were on her, and the looks in those eyes de-
manded an explanation.

She held out her open palm so that all the men could
see what she had found.

"What do you think these are?" she asked.

"Toothpicks?" the SEAL commander said. "They
probably had olives on the end of them and were floating in martinis at one time."

"I suppose that qualifies as a good guess. But have
you noticed that each little stick is a different length?
Does that ring any bells?"

Bolan smiled. "They're lots, aren't they?"

Harmon lit up, warming to the neat piece of deduc-
tion she was working through in her head.

"Yes, exactly! Lots! They were drawing lots and this
poor schmuck lost the draw."

"Lots?" the SEAL commander repeated. "Why in
hell would these people draw lots just so one of them
could be laid out on this table and carved up like a holiday ham? What kind of crazy people would do that?"

"That's your first mistake, Commander. These people aren't crazy. From inside their minds, they're the
most rational and aware group of people on the planet

today. They have very passionate beliefs about how the universe works and where humans fit into that cosmic picture. They are looking at the world using a magical model rather than a scientific one."

"You mean this guy was chosen to be a sacrifice?"

"More than just a sacrifice. Within many primitive world views, particularly among African religions like voodoo and its Latin American offshoots, there is a method of divining the future by examining the entrails of freshly killed chickens or goats or other small animals."

"You mean they killed this guy and pulled his guts out so they could tell the future?"

"That's essentially what I'm saying, yes."

"That's not crazy, that's goddamn insane."

"To us, it's insane. To these people though, it's religion."

This was the second time the Executioner had worked with the agent from the BSU. While the ideas she was advocating in that first encounter seemed extreme and even a little off the wall, he recognized something in her that he knew very well—because that same fire was burning in his soul, keeping him warm at night.

The woman was a crusader. So was Bolan.

Bolan's instincts were sometimes wrong. His instinct about Mallory Harmon was to listen to her. She just might have a piece of the puzzle that the Executioner had always lacked. Bolan had been fighting human evil for most of his adult life now. He knew the face of human evil. He knew that reptilian leer all too well. But did evil begin and end only in the human heart, the human mind? Or was there something…else?

Bolan studied the face of the dead man. There was no horror there. No terror of the unknown or of the finality of death. This guy made the jump to the other side willingly. Bolan understood that kind of fevered dedication, that absolute belief that canceled all doubt, all hesitation, and all attachment to life itself.

The man's arms were outstretched and his smile was so clenched, death couldn't break through to release and relax that mask.

"Why did they feel they needed to perform this ritual in the first place? Any ideas about that question?" Bolan asked.

Harmon thought about that.

"Murphy's Law short-circuited something that had been believed to be of divine providence, something that couldn't be sidestepped but was. They found that fate might be as uncertain as anything else in this universe. To their belief system, where nothing happens by chance and events can be preordained before the foundations of the universe were laid, that's a pretty heavy shock to have to take all at once. They needed to know what this was the harbinger of. They had to know how it was going to change things, change their plans."

"You can't read guts, can you?"

"No, but I'm certain that whatever they saw in this man's intestines disturbed them even more. So much that they just abandoned this tub and ran back to their sanctuary, their sacred place, because these events are an attack on the very center of everything they believe."

Bolan summed it up in terms he was more comfortable with. "The playing field has changed and they're huddling, wondering what to do about it."

"Boy, you men really do catch on to things once you translate it into football," Harmon said.

As Bolan had deduced, the yacht was deserted except for the body of the man in the main dining room. The raiding party returned to the lower deck and the Jet Ski garage. Bolan retrieved a black rubber bag about the size of a gym bag and told the SEAL commander, "I have to send a private communication to my people. I'll be back in a minute."

"What's wrong with going through the Pentagon?"

"We like to keep our higher-up informed directly."

He had to put in a call to home before the sweep went ashore.

16

The white Cape Cod-style house was three stories tall and completely devoid of human habitation. The floor-by-floor sweep went quickly and without incident. In the pantry located off the kitchen, they found a secret door in a false wall that revealed a flight of stairs that disappeared down into the moist, clammy darkness of the underground. That dank air was tinged with the suggestion of ammonium.

The SEAL-SOG task force knew what that meant.

The soldiers went down into a nightmare and brought the war back to the devil.

It was a victory of sorts, a very minor one when the big picture was considered.

The Executioner knew that shutting down the Bermuda branch of this nameless cult amounted to something like a pinprick on the hide of a much larger beast.

There would be other battles in places all over the globe.

The War Everlasting had no end in sight.

THEY'VE THWARTED A GOD, Wesson Fairchild thought. He watched the tall figure dressed in black, chest-heavy with personal munitions stalking toward him through the smoke and firelight. This one was a human devil. He seemed to exist solely to oppose evil men. He and his minions had challenged the will of the Dreaming One and had emerged victorious.

The price for failure was always death.

Fairchild had a standing procedure to be followed in such an event. His master had made it very clear that failure of the cult's leader was the failure of the cult and sentence would be carried out against all of them. When the avatar was killed, the cult's failure in protecting a chosen vessel sealed their doom. The sacrifice of the accountant for divination purposes made it even clearer: only one thing could atone for this blunder. Blood and bone ground into gruel. Every one of them—fodder. Food for the avatar-to-be.

To the cultists, the sentence wasn't something to fear or feel shame over. It was a great honor to become fuel for a monstrous life-form groomed to incarnate the soul of a banished god. Even in death, the cultists would be providing the master with a great service.

Fairchild was the last man in line to make that final departure, like the captain of a ship. The thirty members of the Concealed Order had already thrown themselves off the hexagon-shaped platform of poured concrete and into the waters of the underground lagoon. It was ritual suicide, and Fairchild was to be the thirty-first.

But he waited, measuring the time in heartbeats as another kind of avatar crossed the bridge from sandy shore and onto the platform that was the place of holy sacrifice. From opposite ends of this giant altar, two extremes of cosmic force eyeballed the other in an appraisal that was both contemptuous and yet understanding. The two men both understood the other's pedigree and respected the purity of that presence.

Fairchild thought it was funny that this bastard crusader would choose the color black as his symbolic badge of office.

That diamond-hard gaze staring him down was completely uncompromising.

No pacts were to be made with this devil.

"I salute you," Fairchild said. "Your subterfuge came as a complete surprise. You might have beaten us but you cannot prevail against *him*."

Bolan's grim features cracked a death's-head grin. "I've been prevailing for a long time now."

"Indeed."

"You're just another crazy branch off the same cannibal tree I've been pruning. The hocus-pocus is impressive, but I've got mojo of my own."

"But you are just a man."

"And so are you. But you are a dead man."

It broke the surface of the water behind the devil priest like a great black uprooted tree. The whip arm of the beast coiled and struck.

The Executioner was faster. The Desert Eagle swung up into target acquisition and exploded with one thundering roar. The rhomboid paddle of flesh tipping the whip arm, bristling with bony claws jutting from sucker disks, was cupped to make the sweep back into the water with another tender morsel in its grasp. The supersonic projectile made contact with head bone with time to spare.

In a send-off of bloody fireworks, Wesson Fairchild was poleaxed backward into the writhing Medusa's nest of hunger.

The Executioner holstered his weapon in thigh leather and jerked a baseball grenade off his assault vest, advancing on the real enemy here. The stench of ammonia was gagging. He squinted and held his breath against the chemical onslaught. He yanked the pin out with his teeth and overhanded the bomb into the churning blood-red waters.

The water erupted in a geyser of foam and foulness. He pulled and primed another grenade and another and another. He didn't stop until there were no more grenades left to pull off his vest.

As the blasted waters settled back into smoothness, Bolan stalked up to the lip of the platform and peered into the cloudy deep.

It was dead, but its soul wasn't.

He felt the presence of something evil wash over him, sticky like black tar, then pass. It was like an invisible, slimy tongue taking a taste of a banquet to follow someday. Someday soon.

His eyes narrowed and he wondered.

THE OBELISK WAS a five-sided spike of phallic obscenity and non-Euclidean angles.

Mallory Harmon dropped chest-down into the fine sand and looked for an opening out and around. The seven SEALs were down in front of her in a widely spaced V-wedge, ladling heavy return fire into the line of zombie mind-controlled defenders dug in to defend what had to be the mother lode. Her intuition was raging hard. She had to move now or she'd lose something here that might never be recovered again.

"Cover me!" she yelled. "I'm moving!"

She bounded up out of the sand and bolted off on a wide, looping arch to the right.

Starbuck bellowed, "You dumb—" and bit down on the rest of it. He couldn't stop her. The best thing he could do was to continue firing at them before they could shoot her.

She was possessed. She barely felt her neoprene-clad feet digging into the packed sand as she ran toward what had to be the crossroads of her life's quest. She was an elegant figure in motion, dancing a ballet of determination packing the heat of a Glock .40.

The SEALs covered her move with a vengeance.

She made it to the weird architecture of the stairs that led into the sinister temple. The entrance was more of an orifice, like a hungry maw ready to rend the uninitiated. A yellow-orange glow was coming from in there, reflected torchlight or oil lanterns. She went in without hesitation, leading with the Glock.

One of the zombie parishioners was very busy setting up the means of denying the infidels access to the most coveted secrets of this subterranean religion. A block of C-4 plastique was taped to each of the five sides of the interior walls, which were scrawled with alien hieroglyphics and pictographic symbols that covered the carved masonry from floor to towering apex. Each block of plastique was wired to a blasting cap and daisy-chained into a single electrical firing device. The cultist was connecting the final leads into the initiator when Harmon burst into the inner sanctum.

The youth couldn't have been more than eighteen years old with eyes that burned with pure murder. He whirled to face Harmon and howled like a wolf. He was wearing the same gray coveralls as the rest. He dropped the firing device, snatched a machete off the stone floor next to his feet and leaped at her.

Mallory Harmon didn't hesitate.

The Glock boomed twice. The youth was blown away and pasted to the wall by the full-metal-jacket .40-caliber slugs. It always pained her to have to kill people but in life-or-death showdowns, there was no second place winner.

She retrieved the electric firing device and disarmed the wiring. She chucked the initiator through the entrance for good measure and considered the unholy lectern that dominated the center of the evil room. It was built of stacked human skulls and mortar. Atop the lectern was a very large book, hand-bound and printed. The cover was some kind of leather and as she stepped closer, touching the weird occult symbols embossed into the cover, she had one of those flashes that told the rest of the story.

The cover of this book was made from human skin.

MACK BOLAN WAS moving across the beach toward the obelisk when the earpiece crackled with traffic.

"Striker, this is Jezebel. Would you please join me at the opposite end of this lagoon?"

Bolan looked out across the water toward the farthest reaches of the huge underground cavern. He could see faint firelight out there and the hint of a towering shape, something huge and monstrous, but the distance and the lack of illumination made identification impossible.

"I'm on my way," Bolan responded.

Bolan didn't waste any time. He ran. His long, muscular legs carried him around the edge of the lagoon and into the gloom of the underground grotto. That ominous shape coalesced into a form the closer he got to the dozens of burning tiki torches stuck into the stand in front of the monument.

The seven SEALs and Agent Harmon were standing at the foot of a gigantic statue carved out of some kind of green stone. The sculpture had no reference points in his vast memory.

"Christ," he breathed.

His head was craned back as far as it could go. The thing was that tall.

From whatever order of foulness this thing had lurched, it was bipedal like a man but that's where its anthropomorphism ended. Its head was more like a gigantic squid than an octopus, pointed and arching behind its back. Its eyes weren't symmetrical or lidded. More like poached eggs that had been stepped on and slapped onto a countenance that served as a face. Where a mouth should have been were dozens of writhing tentacles and pseudopods. Its body was bulbous and hinted at being boneless like a gigantic bag of slime. Its arms were long and lean with huge clawed hands that had three digits and an opposable thumb. Its legs were squat and felinelike with clubfeet that had no toes—just five hooked talons instead. And spread out behind it, jutting out of its back were huge, batlike wings that didn't seem to be capable of flight.

Harmon looked over her shoulder at Bolan and said, "You can understand their affinity for *Architeuthis* now, huh?"

The Executioner didn't know what this monument was or what it represented. All he knew was that something had left one goddamned huge footprint right in the middle of the world, which couldn't be ignored or denied.

Epilogue

Los Angeles, California

The two brothers embraced just outside Gate 23 at LAX. The reunion was long overdue. Bolan had come in on the red-eye flight so traffic was sparse and gawking was cut to the bare minimum.

"It's damned good to see you again, Johnny," Mack Bolan said.

The younger Bolan grinned and nodded. "You finally got my messages, huh?"

Bolan had an overnight bag slung over his shoulder. "Yeah. Leo was getting a bit peeved by your insistence."

"This isn't the place to talk."

"You've got that right. Let's find a cold one."

The two Bolan men caught up on lost time as they walked down the deserted concourse and angled into the first lounge they encountered.

A bored but tasty looking blond bartender was reading the first edition of the *Times* as the two men walked up to the bar.

"I'm buying," Bolan said. "What's your poison?"

"Coffee. Very black."

Bolan frowned. "You sure?"

Johnny nodded.

"Well, I need something a little stiffer than that."

It was Johnny's turn to frown and lift a questioning eyebrow. "Yeah? Since when? This isn't normal procedure for you, dude."

"That's right. But things aren't normal right now."

The bartender slowly moved into position to take the order so she could return to the paper.

"What'll it be, guys?"

"A coffee. Very black. And a beer. Something heavy."

"Guinness?"

"Sure. A Guinness. Make it two."

Johnny's other eyebrow shot up. The bartender went to fill the order.

Bolan winked at him and smiled. "Don't worry. I'm not on a binge."

"Well," the younger Bolan said. "I can't wait to hear what has motivated this break from habit for you."

"Yeah. But you first."

The bartender returned with two cans of the dark Irish beverage and one coffee—very black. She rang it up.

"That'll be thirteen dollars please."

Bolan flipped her a twenty.

"Keep the change."

The bartender really warmed to that. "Thank you! You let me know if I can get you anything else!"

Bolan gave her a smile and grabbed the two cans while Johnny took the cup of coffee. Bolan went for the booth with a view of the airfield in the farthest corner of the lounge.

"Two-fisted drinking and throwing taxpayer money around like a corrupt congressman. What's gotten into you, Mack?"

Bolan took a seat on one side of the round table and Johnny scooted in directly across from him. He popped the top on the first can of Guinness and took a deep pull.

"Leo wouldn't get into details because you wouldn't get into details. So what are the details, Johnny?"

"Do you remember back in the midnineties when the *San Jose Sun* broke a story that became a national scandal about how the CIA was peddling crack through Southern California street gangs?"

Bolan nodded. "Yeah. As I remember, the damage control arm of the Company went into overdrive to discredit that one right off the front pages. So?"

"So there was no misinformation in that story at all. The Company really is dealing drugs."

"That's what you called me out here for?"

"Not exactly."

Bolan sipped the Guinness again, waiting.

Johnny continued after blowing on his coffee and testing it for temperature. The temperature was good, so he slugged down a quarter of the cup.

"A woman came running into my office three days ago with a pack of black gangbangers contracted for snatch ops hot on her heels. I defused the situation and got the girl to a safehouse where I could get her story."

"You defused the situation?"

"Right."

"Define defused."

"I nuked them with CS and called a cop friend of mine to send in the squad cars for mop up. I know you would have handled it differently. But that's you, not me."

The Executioner chuckled at his younger brother's words.

"Go on."

"Well, questioning the woman didn't get me anywhere. She had no idea why these thugs were trying to grab her. So I went through my cop friend again, pulled the jackets on the hoods who had tried to grab her and nailed down which set these boys belonged to and went after the ringleader."

"Solid strategy," Bolan commented. "Climb the chain of command until you can't climb any higher."

"Right. And without killing anybody, either."

"The wonders of a liberal education."

It was Johnny's turn to chuckle.

"Hey, I've got to get the digs in. It's not like you stay in touch."

"You know why I stay away."

Johnny pursed his lips and looked down into his cup. "I understand, sure. But it would be nice to hear from you once in a while."

Bolan felt the awkward pause and didn't want to go there.

"What did the gang leader know?"

"He knew a federal agent working in the DEA. This agent suggested it would be good for his street business if he sent a few of his boys to get my client and bring her to him."

"It didn't end there though, did it?"

"Oh, hell no. The Fed was just a cutout working for the real man."

"Uh-huh. That's the way spooks do business."

"I ended up smoking out a respected banker named Dixon Higgs. You ever heard of the guy?"

"Never."

"Higgs is more than just a banker. He was educated at Georgetown and was recruited into the Company right before graduation. He comes from a family of bankers and the Company wanted a bank. You can guess why they might want to own a bank lock, stock and barrel."

Bolan nodded. "Sure. To launder the drug money and then loan it out to make even more money on the interest."

"Bingo. To finance more black ops off the books and out of reach of congressional oversight."

"So how does the woman fit into all of this?"

"Her brother."

"What about him?"

"Her brother was compelled, shall we say, to join the ultimate drug coup to bankroll Company fun and games. He's a notorious meth cook who happened to make it big through the cowboy days of crank. Well, he made it to the other side, retired and was never caught. He's developed a revolutionary method of cooking meth that could put the war on drugs out of business. He refused to go back into the game but they made him do it anyway. The woman was to act as insurance to keep him overseeing the crank operation. If he didn't keep the pipeline flowing, she was going to be hurt."

Bolan knew this story already.

"This guy writes books in the underground press, doesn't he?"

"Yeah. Manuals on drug manufacturing."

"His pen name is Uncle Martin."

"How did you know that?"

"Because I ran into him out there."

"You were in Cassiopeia?"

"That's where I've been."

"You shut it down, then."

Bolan took a moment to find the right words. Finally

he said, "A lot of different interests converged out there to bring the curtain down."

"Where's Uncle Martin now? You didn't kill him, did you?"

Bolan shook his head. "No. The DEA has got him. I'd guess they'll be debriefing him for some time to come."

Johnny could see it in his brother's eyes. The early-morning drinking, the haunted edges and echoes in his voice. "What happened out there, Mack?"

Bolan took several more swallows of his drink before he even considered getting into that side of it.

"You've heard of the perfect storm, haven't you?"

Johnny nodded.

"Well, that one wasn't. This one was. I know. I was there to see it."

And then he told the tale.

**In a ruined world, the past and future clash
with frightening force...**

JAMES AXLER

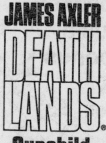

DEATH LANDS ®

Sunchild

Ryan Cawdor and his warrior companions come face-to-face with
the descendants of a secret society who were convinced that
paradise awaited at the center of the earth. This cult is inexorably
tied to a conspiracy of twentieth-century scientists devoted to
fulfilling a vision of genetic manipulation. In this labyrinthine ville,
some of the descendants of the Illuminated Ones are pursuing the
dream of their legacy—while others are dedicated to its nightmare.

Even in the Deathlands, twisted human beliefs endure....

Available in December 2001 at your favorite retail outlet.

GOLD EAGLE ®

GDL56

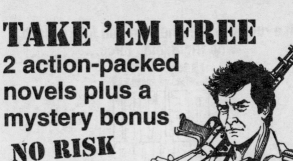

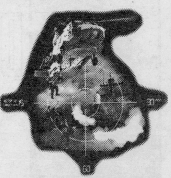